# SUPERGRANNY

## THE CHARACTER
## WHO CAME TO LIFE

A fa... prob-
len... ome
to ...

S... ay to
hel... kids,
Sh... man
wh... o life
...

 printed on recycled paper

 PRINTED WITH
SOY INK

## Supergranny Mysteries

Supergranny 1: The Mystery of the Shrunken Heads
ISBN 0-916761-16-9
Library Hardcover: ISBN 0-916761-17-7

Supergranny 2: The Case of The Riverboat Riverbelle
ISBN 0-916761-08-8
Library Hardcover: ISBN 0-916761-09-6

Supergranny 3: The Ghost of Heidelberg Castle
ISBN 0-916761-06-1
Library Hardcover: ISBN 0-916761-07-X

Supergranny 4: The Secret of Devil Mountain
ISBN 0-916761-04-5
Library Hardcover: ISBN 0-916761-05-3

Supergranny 5: The Character Who Came to Life
ISBN 0-916761-18-5
Library Hardcover: ISBN 0-916761-19-3

Supergranny 6: The Great College Caper
ISBN 0-916761-14-2
Library Hardcover: ISBN 0-916761-15-0

---

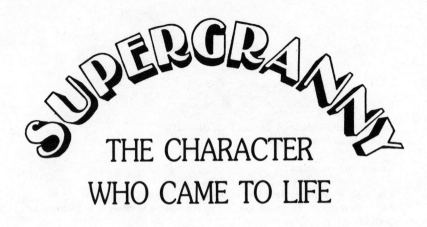

# SUPERGRANNY

# THE CHARACTER
# WHO CAME TO LIFE

Beverly Hennen Van Hook

Holderby & Bierce

Published by Holderby & Bierce, P.O. Box 4296,
Rock Island, IL 61201-4296

Andrea Nelken, editor

Paperback. ISBN: 0-916761-18-5
Library Hardcover. ISBN 0-916761-19-3

SUMMARY: A famous Chicago mystery writer summons Supergranny's help when
the villain in her book *seems* to come alive. From the lake front, Art Institute,
Chicago Public Library and Brookfield Zoo to the El and a secret room above a
Loop supper club, it's nonstop adventure for the elderly detective and pals. Fifth
in the series.

Holderby & Bierce, October, 1989
2nd Printing, September, 1992

Printed in the U.S.A.

To Mom and Dad Van Hook

# 1

"We'll move fast and have a plan," Supergranny said as she drove the Ferrari along the Congress Parkway that morning at 50 miles per hour, bumper to bumper, center lane.

"No way are we going to wander around Chicago, willy-nilly, then kick ourselves for missing so much when we get home," she said.

Supergranny, also known as Sadie Geraldine Oglepop, is our next-door neighbor. She was treating me — along with my older sister, Angela, and my younger sister, Vannie — to a fast few days in Chicago.

We'd also brought our Old English sheepdog, Shackleford, who pouts for a week if we leave her behind. And, of course, we had Supergranny's mini-robot, Chesterton, who'd do a lot worse than pout if we dared go off without *him*.

I say a "fast few days" because Supergranny looooooves Chicago and thinks it's a sin to let its good parts go to waste when she's in town.

"Review the Hit List, Joshua," Supergranny said to me, as the Ferrari shot under the post office into downtown.

I was in charge of the Hit List of things we wanted to do this trip. I fished it out of my pocket and started reading from the top with the "regulars."

The "regulars" are the absolute favorite things Supergranny does every time she visits Chicago. They go like this:

## Chicago Hit List
### Regulars

1. Rent bikes and cruise Lake Shore.
2. Have tea at Mayfair Regent Hotel with Victoria Charmain.
3. Watch poisonous frogs at Brookfield Zoo.
4. Visit "Paris, A Rainy Day" at Art Institute.

I moved on to "Major Optionals." There are 147 Major Optionals and the idea is to knock ourselves out and run ourselves ragged doing as many as possible.

They go like this:

## Major Optionals

1. Rest of Art Institute
2. Cubs game
3. Field Museum
4. Aquarium
5. Museum of Science and Industry
6. Water Tower Place
7. Bears game
8. Schubert show

9. White Sox game
10. Ballet
11. Tribune and Sun-Times newspaper tours
12. Cheeseburger at Billy Goat Tavern
13. Top of John Hancock and/or Sears Tower
14. "El" train (named because part of its track is "elevated" in the air)

That's as far as I got before we pulled up to the Barclay Hotel to check in while the valet parked the Ferrari.

Our suite was just like the motels we stay in with Mom and Dad, except that it had a kitchen, two televisions, a sunken living room, a picture window overlooking Lake Michigan, a big basket of flowers, and a room service menu with champagne, pizza, and corned beef hash.

Angela, Vannie and I took one look at the suite and forgot the Hit List.

"Let's just relax here and order pizza," I suggested.

"Fresh flowers," Angela marveled. "A humongous basket of fresh flowers. With a note: 'Welcome Back, Sadie.' "

Meanwhile Vannie was banging around the kitchen, checking every cabinet and drawer and yelling things like, "Oh, wow, a bottle opener! And a brown refrigerator! And honey-roasted peanuts!

"Why go anywhere?" she asked Supergranny. "We've got everything right here."

"Good idea," Angela chimed in. "Let's just stick around and enjoy the suite. We can ride bikes at home." She stuck her nose back into the flowers. "I could get used to this. I AM used to it. Already."

For once, I agreed with them.

Why rush off to some museum after five short minutes

of luxury? Wouldn't the museum still be there next time? Where would a ten thousand-ton marble museum with solid bronze lions GO?

It was no good.

Supergranny had already unpacked and was fastening her helmet.

"We'll come back to sleep," she said briskly, heading for the elevator.

We trailed after her.

Onward to our rented bikes and No. 1 on the Hit List. Onward to tea at the Mayfair with world-famous mystery writer Victoria Charmain.

And, unknown to us, onward to a few things that weren't on the Hit List. A secret supper above a Loop[1] cafe. A strange and sinister letter. And a race through the flickering shadows beneath the El.

\*         \*         \*         \*

Chicago is a city where you can lie on the sand and look at the skyscrapers.

Just walk a couple of blocks from Michigan Avenue, cut through a tunnel under Lake Shore Drive, and — wham! — beach time.

One minute you're surrounded by banks, stores, offices, Brooks Brothers suits, limousines and traffic jams. Next minute, by sand, Coppertone, picnickers, runners, bikers, skaters, loafers, lovers, gulls and Lake Michigan stretching out for miles to meet the sky.

We hopped on the bikes and headed north along the lake, with Supergranny in the lead. Next came Angela and

-------------------

1. Section of downtown Chicago where the El makes a loop.

Vannie with Chesterton in a basket. I brought up the rear holding Shackleford's leash, which wasn't easy and probably was impossible.

At first, Shackleford was all fired up and took off at Mach 2. Luckily, she wound down before we wiped out, but then she remembered she was bashful and shied from a guy videotaping his baby.

She veered to his left as I passed him on the right, and I let go of the leash just in time. One microsecond later and we'd have lassoed him, video camera and all.

Shackleford bounded ahead to tailgate Supergranny, and I focused on the curving line of blue lake, skyscrapers and light blue sky. And on not hitting a major crack and catapulting off the ledge into the water.

After about 2½ miles, Supergranny pulled off near Lincoln Park Beach. We locked the bikes and waded in the lake a while before taking off for Victoria Charmain's on foot.

"We're so close we might as well stop by," Supergranny said. "To confirm tea."

"You mean her house?" Angela asked breathlessly. "We're ACTUALLY going to her HOUSE? Where she LIVES???"

She was gushier about it than Vannie and I because she'd read some of Victoria Charmain's books. They're adult mysteries and Vannie and I haven't gotten around to them yet.

Angela, of course, has.

In fact, she'd done a report on Charmain, which isn't surprising because Angela has done a report on every subject in the world and gotten at least an A- on each of them.

This report was on "Four Famous Black Female Writers"

and we knew all about it because she told us all about it on the three-hour drive from home.

"I did a report on her, you know," she said as we crossed a footbridge over Lake Shore Drive.

"We know," Vannie said. "And on Gwendolyn Brooks Lauren."

"Laureate," Angela said. "Gwendolyn Brooks, poet laureate of Illinois."

"Right," Vannie said.

"And Alice Walker," I said. "And . . ."

"Maya Angelou," Supergranny put in.

"Yes," Angela said. "And Gwendolyn Brooks lives in Chicago, too."

"We know," I said.

"You told us," Vannie said.

"She's won a Pulitzer prize and Victoria Charmain has won three Edgars, a *very* fancy mystery writing prize, and they live right here in our own state and have probably walked on these very sidewalks and . . ."

Once Angela starts reciting a report, you're in for it. She'll go on for years. But this was really unfair because we'd just heard the whole thing in detail for three hours in the car.

"Stop her, Supergranny," Vannie begged.

"Please," I said. "I know it by heart already."

Angela got ticked. "Well, SOME people would AP-PRECIATE being briefed before they meet a famous author," she huffed. "I'm just trying to help you be IN-FORMED so you won't act like ILLITERATE BAR-BARIANS when you meet her!"

"Then let's compromise, Angela," Supergranny said. "Give us a test. Four questions."

"Test?" Angela asked.

"Sure," Supergranny answered.

"On Four Famous Black Female Writers?" Angela asked.

"Sure," Supergranny answered.

"I pick the questions?" Angela asked.

"You're the teacher," Supergranny answered. "If we flunk, you may give the entire report again even if it takes till Christmas.

"Deal," Angela said. "One: Who wrote 'The Color Purple'?"

"Alice Walker!" Vannie yelled. "Easy."

"Murder weapon in Victoria Charmain's 'Phantom Cliffs'?"

"Bats!" I yelled.

"What kind of bats? Baseball bats?" Angela asked, trying to trick me.

"No. Ugly little flying mammals," I yelled. "The murderer put them in a picnic basket in the victim's car, and when it got dark they flew out of the basket and the victim panicked and drove off the cliff."

"Excellent, Joshua," Angela said. "Number three: What famous female writer is also a singer, dancer and actress?"

"Maya Angelou!" Supergranny shouted. "She acted in 'Porgy and Bess,' danced with the Martha Graham Company and did a thousand other things."

"Very good," Angela said. By then we'd reached the Charmains' row house and sat on the steps to finish the test.

"Match point," Angela said. "Who wrote 'The Bean Eaters' and 'We Real Cool'?"

"Gwendolyn Brooks!" I shouted.

"Congratulations," Angela said. "No report."

Vannie and I cheered so loud, a next-door neighbor pulled back a curtain to see what the ruckus was about. Supergranny went up the steps and rang the bell beside the old-fashioned oak door. We all crowded onto the stoop and peered through the long, glass, door panels into the hall.

The left wall had a coat rack with about a hundred coats, jackets and Cubs caps, an umbrella stand with a bunch of umbrellas and a walking stick, and a steep staircase with books and magazines stacked along the railing side.

The right wall had a gigantic painting of a rocking chair with the head of a woman. That's right — a rocking chair body with the head of a woman.

A tall, thin woman appeared out of the shadows at the end of the hall. Slowly she walked toward us. Her face peered through the glass. It was the face in the painting. The painting of the rocking chair with the head of a woman.

# 2

"Oh no," the woman said, opening the door and pulling us inside. "You've missed her."

She gave Supergranny a quick peck on the cheek and frowned.

"Something strange has happened, and she's anxious to talk to you. She didn't want to wait until tea.

"I told her, 'Victoria, phone first. You know Sadie, she'll be out of that hotel in five minutes, roller-skating down State Street or chartering a salmon boat.'

"But you know Victoria with a bee in her bustle. You can't tell her squat. Off she went in a cab. 'Victoria, you'll miss her,' I said.

"Well, she missed you. Here you are and there she is off in a cab. Maybe I can catch her if I ring your hotel.

"Show your friends the gallery and I'll be right back," the woman said, motioning toward the next room. "There are root-beer barrel candies in the coffeepot." She melted back into the shadows.

"Olivia," Supergranny whispered as we walked into the

9

room. "She's Victoria's sister. She ran an art gallery in Paris for years until she retired back here to live with Victoria. Six weeks into retirement she was so bored she was driving Victoria bonkers, so they turned the first floor into a gallery and she's back in business. They live on the top two floors."

The gallery had 11-foot-high white walls filled with paintings, dark woodwork, a couch, and a desk with a coffeepot and a bunch of art magazines on top. A gargantuan rubber plant that looked like a people-eater was in the front bay window and a gargantuan painting of a coffeepot hung over the mantle.

The coffeepot seemed to float in space and was polished to reflect the room. Standing in front of it you could see the reflection of the hall stairs and coats, jackets, Cubs caps, umbrellas and the walking stick behind what you thought was a reflection of you until you looked closer and saw it was a reflection of Olivia Charmain.

"Wow, it's painted to look like a reflection," Angela whispered. "Painted by someone who knows the room. Someone named 'Lionel,' " she said, squinting at the artist's tiny signature.

"Weird," Vannie said.

"Thirty-seven thousand," I said, pulling a tag on a string from behind a lower corner of the painting. "It's for sale for $37,000."

"I'll take it," Angela said.

We all laughed as Olivia Charmain walked back into the room.

"Well, it's too late. Your hotel says she has been and gone," she said.

"We could wait here for her," Supergranny said. "I

10

mean, we're due at the Brookfield in a half-hour, but if it's important we'd be happy to —"

"No point in that," Olivia cut in briskly, passing around the coffeepot from the desk.

It was full of root-beer barrels. We each took one.

"No point in waiting because she has some mysterious errand or other and won't be back until after your tea," Olivia said.

"So we ARE still on for tea?" Supergranny asked, trying to talk around the root-beer barrel in her mouth.

"Most decidedly, dear. It's all she talked about this morning. At the Mayfair. Four o'clock. If you're not there she'll skin you.

"In fact, she left you a note in case she missed you. Let's see, where did she put it — oh, yes. Young man, would you be so kind as to bring me my ebony walking stick from the hall?"

I got the walking stick, which was black with a gold Wrigley Building on top.

She shook it. "Yes, it's in there all right." She unscrewed the gold Wrigley Building, took it off, and turned the walking stick upside down. An envelope fell out.

"It says 'SADIE,' " Vannie said, handing the envelope to Supergranny.

Supergranny tore open the envelope, read the note and frowned. Then she read it again. And frowned.

"Oh, my, I am sorry we missed her. Olivia . . . ," she said slowly, "did Victoria tell you anything about this 'mysterious errand'?"

Olivia shrugged. "Not one word. And she's been sashaying around like this for days, not telling a soul what she's up to.

" 'What's worrying you, Victoria?' I keep asking. 'Spill it.' But will she tell me? Not a word. She says she won't tell me because I'm too high-strung, go off the deep end, fall apart, get hysterical and panic at the first sign of trouble.

" 'Victoria, I'm cool as lime punch,' I tell her. 'What's going on?'

"But she won't talk. Says it's not important anyway. Phone calls at 2 a.m. Nervous as a squirrel with hives. Then she has the nerve to tell me it's not important.

"Another week of this, Sadie, and I'm heading straight back to France.

"And I don't want to run you out," she added, not stopping to breathe, "but if you plan to be at the Brookfield in a half-hour, you'd better call a cab. At that you'll probably be an hour late. And I'd advise you to leave that robot and dog with me. They might spook the animals. A zoo riot is the last thing Chicago needs."

We weren't crazy about spooking any lions and rhinoceroses ourselves, so we agreed to leave Shackleford and Chesterton with her and called a cab.

We waved goodbye to them and Olivia, piled into the cab and took off for Brookfield Zoo.

"Now will you tell us?" Angela asked.

"The note," Vannie said. "What was in the note?"

"Nothing new, really," Supergranny said. "Nothing Olivia hadn't told us, really . . . but Olivia tends to get upset so easily, that I wasn't really concerned until I saw it in Victoria's own hand."

She pulled the note out of her sweatsuit pocket and passed it around.

"Urgent. Must see you. Confirm tea: Mayfair. 4 p.m. Don't alarm Olivia. Can't handle stress, you know. VC."

# 3

"What frogs?" Vannie asked.

"I don't see any frogs," Angela said.

We were standing in front of a lighted case in the Brookfield Zoo reptile house.

"Keep watching," Supergranny said.

"Dendrobates auraatus," Angela read. "Poison arrow frogs."

"It just looks like a case of rocks, plants and gravel to me," I said.

"Keep watching," Supergranny said.

"Just rocks, plants, gravel and those pretty, little, green and black stones," Vannie said.

"They look like polished marble," Angela said. "Like green and black, polished marble chips."

"Or jewels," Vannie said. "From a rich lady's ring."

Boinnnng. Something had happened in the case. One of the green and black marble chips disappeared. One second there it was on a pile of rocks. The next — vanished.

Boinnnnggg. I shook my head and refocused my eyes.

Something was going on in that case. Two marble chips were sitting on a little branch that was empty seconds before. I could have SWORN it was empty a second before. I'd testify IN COURT it was empty seconds before.

"HEY!" Vannie yelled, pointing at the case with her mouth open.

Good. I wasn't the only one. Vannie saw it, too.

"HEY!" Angela yelled, pointing at the case with her mouth open. It was an epidemic, I thought. An epidemic of people pointing at this case with their mouths opened. I was enjoying how stupid they looked when suddenly I realized I was doing it, too. I shut my mouth and stopped pointing.

"Boiiinnnng." A little chip zinged across the case.

"Boiinnnng." There went another one.

"Boiinnnng, boiing, boiiing." They were bouncing around the case like flying jewels.

"Good night, they're alive," Angela said.

"And fast as fleas," I said.

"Or jumping beans," Vannie added.

Supergranny laughed. "They're frogs. Deadly little fingernail-sized frogs. South American Indians used to extract their poison to use on arrow tips."

"Ugh, gross," Vannie said.

"But fascinating," Angela added.

"I agree," Supergranny said. "Terrible, but fascinating. That's why I visit them every time I come to Chicago. Of course, it's more fun if you can bring someone along who hasn't seen them before.

"Last time I brought Victoria. I had a devil of a time getting her to stand here long enough to see the frogs perform. I thought they never were going to jump around.

14

Victoria almost took off for the giraffes.

"Of course, when they did start she was hooked and wouldn't leave. I wouldn't be a bit surprised to see these frogs turn up in one of her mysteries."

"I can see it now," Angela said. "A mysterious letter with frog juice in the envelope glue."

"One lick and — clunk!" Vannie fell backward, pretending to choke from licking an envelope laced with poisonous frog juice.

"WATCH IT!" a man behind us yelled as she knocked him down and fell on him.

Vannie tried to apologize as we helped both of them up, but he just scowled and limped hurriedly away.

"I'm sorry," Vannie kept saying. "I didn't know he was there."

"He was so quiet," I said.

"And standing so close," Vannie said. "Did YOU know he was there?"

We all shook our heads.

"I hadn't seen him since we left Victoria Charmain's," Angela said.

We all stared at her.

"Didn't you notice him as we pulled away?" Angela asked. "He was on the sidewalk hailing a cab."

True, it seemed a little odd that out of Chicago's three million people, the same guy Angela saw in front of Charmain's would turn up at the poisonous frogs.

But we were too busy to think much about it at the time.

"We're running late," Supergranny said as we left the reptile house. "We BARELY have time to pick up Shackleford and Chesterton, grab our bikes, get back to the Barclay and change in time to meet Victoria for tea."

15

"You mean this is it for the zoo?" I asked.

"What about the other 659 animals?" Angela asked.

"Like the polar bears, gorillas and giraffes?" Vannie asked.

"And the ostriches, baboons and anacondas — snakes that can swallow a man whole if his shoulders aren't too big?" I asked.

"And the okapi, quetzals, and Tasmanian devils," Angela asked.

We stared at her. Where does she *get* this stuff? But we didn't ask because she'd probably done a report on weird, little-known animals and was busting to tell us.

Supergranny laughed. "Don't worry. We'll be back."

But after a quick look at her watch, she reconsidered. "On second thought, maybe we *could* squeeze in one animal for each of you.

"But pick one fast," she said, sitting on a bench and handing me a red marker from her purse.

"Joshua, mark an X by your animal on our zoo map."

I picked ostriches and marked an X by "Birds," then passed the map and marker to Vannie.

"Oh, brother. I can't decide between the polar bears and seals," Vannie said.

"Try, Vannie. We haven't got a week," Supergranny said.

"Well, if they're *feeding* the seals, I want to choose them, but, on the other hand, if the polar bears are dunking each other in their pool . . ."

"We'll get back to you, Vannie," Supergranny said with a sigh. "Give the map to Angela."

"Easy," Angela said, marking the giraffes. Angela is a great admirer of giraffes. She read somewhere that they

16

never attack, but can defend themselves against any animal in the wild.

"If everybody were like that, the world would be a whole lot better off," she's always saying. "And war would be out for sure. Done. Finished. Finito. For sure."

"Vannie?" Supergranny asked. "We're back to you."

The old clock was ticking away, and Vannie still couldn't make up her so-called mind about an animal. Worse, she couldn't even keep her so-called mind on the subject because she kept getting distracted by a bush.

"There's something in that bush behind us," she whispered.

"Don't change the subject. Pick an animal," Supergranny ordered.

"I'm not kidding," Vannie said. "I heard it. The bush behind our bench."

"Flip a coin, Joshua," Supergranny said.

"See, the bush leaves are wiggling," Vannie insisted.

"Probably a bird. Is heads polar bears or seals?" Supergranny asked.

"Polar bears," Vannie called the toss, her eyes still glued to the bush.

I flipped. "Heads!" I yelled.

"Polar bears!" Angela yelled.

"Finally," Supergranny sighed, drawing a red line from our bench to birds to giraffes to polar bears to exit, then jumping up.

"Ladies and gentleman, start your engines," she announced, Indy 500 race-announcer style. Then she took off, with us trailing behind.

"I tell you, there's something in that bush," Vannie muttered.

17

"Don't look now, but there he is again," Angela whispered.

We'd just left the zoo and she, Vannie and I were waiting in a cab at Charmain's while Supergranny picked up Shackleford and Chesterton.

"The Poison-Frog Man," Angela said. "In that cab right behind us."

I casually glanced sideways as the cab slowly passed. All I could see was the back of a passenger's head.

"Angela thinks she saw Poison-Frog Man again," Vannie announced as Supergranny climbed into our cab with Shackleford and Chesterton, who reeked of root-beer barrels. "The one I knocked down."

But Supergranny was too miffed at Olivia to pay attention.

"Olivia means well, but I *specifically* asked her not to let them get into those root-beer barrels," she grumbled.

"All we need is for Shackleford to get an upset stomach. You KNOW what happens when she doesn't stick to dog food. And we're darned lucky Chesterton didn't choke."

Chesterton, as you may know, is fueled by gumdrops you stuff into a sensor that looks like a coffee cup on top of his head. Hard candy like root-beer barrels isn't good for him.

"Darned lucky he didn't choke," she repeated. "Olivia said she chopped them up, but still —"

We pulled onto Lake Shore Drive and she forgot all about the root-beer barrels because the same cab darted out of a side street and pulled into the traffic one car behind us.

"See," Angela said, raising her eyebrows. "What did I

tell you?"

"First, Angela sees him outside Charmain's," Vannie said, holding up one finger. "Then he's lurking behind us at the frogs," she adds, holding up a second finger.

"And I'd bet you the Wrigley Building he's what Vannie noticed in that bush," Angela said.

"But why?" I asked. "Why would a stranger be following us?"

"I don't know, but I don't like it," Supergranny said slowly. "It's time we lost him. We'll use Plan 328X.

"Angela, you take Chesterton and the cab driver.

"Joshua and Vannie, you take the bicycle locks.

"I'll handle Shackleford.

"Got it?" she asked.

We nodded as the cab pulled into the Lincoln Park Beach parking lot.

"Good," she said. "GO!"

— Angela popped Chesterton into her backpack and handed the driver a five-dollar bill. "Please keep the change," she said crisply.

— I jumped out the right rear door, raced to our bikes and twirled the combination locks on my bike and Angela's.

— Vannie jumped out the left rear door, raced to the other bikes and twirled the combinations.

In one minute and forty seconds the bikes were unlocked and we were tearing south along the lake with Shackleford barking like a maniac as she ran behind.

I glanced over my shoulder. It was Poison-Frog Man, all right. He'd jumped out of his cab and stood with his hands in his pockets, scowling after us as we sped away.

## 4

We made it to the Mayfair Regent with six minutes to spare and sat at our table, waiting for Victoria Charmain.

Vannie and Supergranny sat on a little white couch, and Angela and I sat in cushioned chairs with curved wooden legs. We saved the pink velvet armchair for Ms. Charmain.

One look at the room and I was awfully glad we left Shackleford and Chesterton back at the Barclay watching Andy Griffith reruns on TV. They are *not* ready for tea at the Mayfair.

"Genteel," Angela said. "That's how I'd describe this. Veddy, veddy genteel."

Angela, as you may know, is forever hitting on a word and using the life out of it before moving on to something new, so I figured we were in for a bellyful of "genteel."

But I had to admit it fit.

You take a humongous room and throw in plenty of white woodwork, thick carpet and long pink drapes; add a grand piano and crystal chandelier; line the walls with Japanese garden scenes and colossal arched mirrors; fill it with little white couches and velvet easy chairs grouped around low tables with linen tablecloths; bring in people in clothes that don't wrinkle and have them talk quietly and make little tinkling laughs and serve them 104 different kinds of fancy mini-rolls and cakes and 37 different kinds of tea in flowered china teapots with quilted covers on them . . . and genteel is as good a word as any.

Into this swept Victoria Charmain.

She was five feet ten if she was an inch. She had broad, straight shoulders and she wore a grand purple hat and a gray cape that billowed in her wake.

Gentlemen jumped up to shake her hand and ladies leaned forward for her to kiss their cheeks while they whispered things that made her break into a Pearl Bailey smile and then into laughter that rolled through the room like a waterfall.

"Wow," Vannie said.

"Dramatic," Angela said.

"You can see why I never miss tea at the Mayfair with Victoria," Supergranny whispered. "But don't let the theatrics fool you. Underneath she's steady as a bank president."

"Stop whispering about me, Sadie, and give me a hug," Ms. Charmain said, swooping down on us.

She hugged Supergranny, then towered above us, pointing at Vannie.

"Don't tell me — you're VANNIE," she said.

"And JOSHUA," she said, the pointing finger moving in my direction.

"And ANGELA," she said with a delighted laugh.

She folded into the pink velvet chair and shook the linen napkin to her lap with a flourish.

21

"I've caught up with you at last. Is Sadie running your legs off as usual? And where have you stashed the famous robot and Old English sheepdog?" She lifted the tablecloth and pretended to look under the table for Shackleford and Chesterton.

Then she poured herself a cup of Earl Gray tea and leaned back as if she didn't have a worry in the world.

"Fire away, children," she said. "How's Chicago so far? I want you to call me Victoria and tell me everything you've done and how you like it. And what do you think of Sadie's hideous little poisonous frogs?"

"Not so fast, Victoria," Supergranny interrupted. "The kids know about your note and we can't stand the suspense any longer. Olivia said something strange is happening but you won't tell her what."

"She said you were off on a mysterious errand," Angela said.

"She said you've been getting phone calls at 2 a.m.," I said.

"She said you were as nervous as a squirrel with hives," Vannie said.

"And your note said 'URGENT,' " Supergranny said.

"Well, yes . . . but I hate to dive right into my own troubles," Victoria said.

"Dive," Supergranny ordered.

"Can't it wait?" Victoria asked. "The children and I have just met and I'd hate for them to think I'm one of those self-centered bores who talk only about themselves . . . "

"VICTORIA! ON WITH IT!" Supergranny barked.

Victoria shrugged. "OK, OK, OK. If you insist.

"The trouble started about a month ago. I remember the date because I'd been to my monthly Mayhem Mystery

Writers Club meeting that night and had drunk WAY too much coffee. I'd just gotten to sleep at 2 a.m. when the phone rang.

"At first I couldn't understand whoever it was, because the voice was muffled, as if the caller had his hand in front of his mouth.

"Then I finally DID understand, but I didn't believe what I heard.

"He said . . . ," She paused, replaced the teacup in its saucer and leaned forward.

" '. . . This is Alphonso Bean.'

"Then he hung up."

She leaned back and surveyed us as if we were supposed to look shocked, surprised, scared or something.

But we just looked blank.

Who was Alphonso Bean? I scanned my brain for data on him. A rock star? Cabinet minister? South American dictator?

I came up with zip.

She kept surveying us.

We kept looking blank.

"I'm afraid I don't recognize the name," Supergranny said.

"Er, do YOU know him, Victoria?" Vannie asked.

"Indeed, I do," she answered. "I know Alphonso. I know he's mad; I know he's planning a murder; and I know why.

"And I'm the only person in the world who does know him, because I created him.

"He's the murderer in my next book. I created him and until now I've never told a soul!"

## 5

Victoria Charmain poured us another round of tea and settled back to summarize her next book, *Artist's Revenge.*

It was the story of Alphonso Bean.

Here's her summary:

Several years ago, two promising young artists moved to New York City to seek their fortune. They shared a loft apartment and worked as waiters to support themselves while they tried to break into Big Time Art.

Roderick Blaine was quiet, hard-working and stuck to his schedule:

7:00 a.m.   — Get up.
7:10 a.m.   — Stretching exercises on front stoop.
7:18 a.m.   — Run.
7:40 a.m.   — Shower.
7:50 a.m.   — Shredded wheat, bagels and apple butter, decaf coffee and "The New York Times."
8:00 a.m.   — Brush and floss.

8:05-2 p.m. — Paint.
2-4 p.m.    — Errands. (Monday, dry cleaners.
              Tuesday & Thursday, art supply store.
              Wednesday & Friday, groceries.)
4 p.m.-midnight   — Wait tables.
12:30 a.m.-7 a.m. — Sleep.
Saturday    — Tour art galleries.
Sunday      — Clean loft.

Alphonso Bean was more flamboyant.

He traipsed around to art gallery openings and press interviews wearing jeans, a tuxedo jacket and sandals with a long, white scarf wrapped around his neck, World War I fighter-pilot style.

He was a clown one minute and a grump the next and before long a lot of people didn't like him, but everybody knew him.

He adored going to parties, sleeping till noon and playing practical jokes, which lost him his job at the restaurant.

One night before the restaurant opened, he loosened all the pepper shaker tops. When the customers tried to pepper their food, the tops fell off, wrecking their meals and making them sneeze.

The restaurant manager caught Alphonso in the kitchen watching the dining-room sneezers through the glass in the swinging door. Alphonso was laughing so hard he couldn't even stop when the manager fired him.

That made the manager so mad he fired Roderick, too, because he knew they were roommates and assumed they were in cahoots.

It was totally unfair to Roderick, who had never played a practical joke in his life, but the manager was too enraged to listen to reason.

Roderick got busy pounding the pavement for another waiter's job and finally found one.

But Alphonso figured he'd had enough of the restaurant business. He got busy borrowing money from Roderick and carousing around with some reporters and art critic friends, regaling them with his "pepper caper" story, along with other practical jokes he claimed he'd pulled.

Pretty soon Alphonso's "pepper caper" had made all the newspaper columns. Some stories said it had happened at the Plaza, some said it had happened at The Russian Tea Room and some said it had happened at a swank, unnamed East Side cafe, but ALL of them spelled A L P H O N S O   B E A N right and called him a "talented young artist."

With all the publicity, his career took off. Three things happened:

1. Judges picked one of his paintings as a finalist in their annual "Top Young Artists of New York" exhibit. (They also picked one of Roderick's.)

2. Fortunada Trifle, the skinny and elegant socialite, invited him to be guest of honor at her annual charity banquet and ball.

3. "Post la Trende," the newest gallery in Manhattan, hung his paintings to sell. (The owner also hung a few of Roderick's at Alphonso's request.)

When Roderick tried to thank Alphonso for getting his paintings hung at the "Post la Trende" gallery, Alphonso waved his thanks aside grandly. "Don't mention it, Old Top," he said. "It's small enough payment for all the money I owe you."

Roderick tried to say that while he was grateful for the

26

favor, he still expected Alphonso to repay his loan. But the words stuck in the back of his throat in a great wad of anger that had been building up like a pile of oily rags.

Because the truth was, deep down in the back of his throat, Roderick was becoming murderously angry at Alphonso.

Why?

Well, for starters, because —

He *needed* the money he'd loaned Alphonso.

*He* waited tables all night while Alphonso partied and then slept late.

*He* painted for six hours a day while Alphonso painted for only a few hours a week — when the mood struck and the moon was right.

*He* did the dishes, bought the groceries, cleaned the refrigerator, scrubbed the loft and picked up after Alphonso, who was the Slob Prince of the Western World.

Meanwhile, all the papers ran Alphonso's picture, calling him "talented young artist," and all the papers ignored Roderick.

That was just for starters.

Anyway, Alphonso's grand, "Don't mention it, Old Top" statement lit Roderick's anger like a torch to oily rags.

No wonder he couldn't speak. There was an explosion in his throat.

He choked. He smiled. He went on running at 7:18 a.m. and waiting tables at 4 p.m. and acting normal on the outside.

But inside one angry word burned, out of control . . . sabotage, sabotage, sabotage.

He was going to sabotage Alphonso's career and wreck his life with a simple, insane, three-pronged plan.

1. One night while Alphonso slept, Roderick stole his long, white, World War I fighter pilot-style scarf, crept into the bathroom, and locked the door. He cut the scarf into 100 two-inch squares and hid them under his mattress.

The next afternoon while he was grocery shopping, he bought 10 dozen eggs. He waited across the street from the loft until Alphonso left with friends. Then he raced inside, boiled the eggs, chopped them up, and sewed them into little flat packets in the 100 pieces of silk scarf.

He attached small strips of double-backed tape to each packet and stuck them in his backpack and headed downtown to the "Top Young Artists of New York" exhibit at the Modern Mid-Town Museum.

2. The night of Fortunada Trifle's annual charity ball, Roderick showed up in his waiter's uniform and blended in with the other waiters who had been hired extra for the banquet and ball. Nobody noticed him as he passed out all the salt and pepper shakers. Nobody noticed as he slipped out a side door and disappeared.

3. The night before Alphonso was to deliver three new paintings to "Post la Trende" gallery, Roderick poured starch into all Alphonso's paints, knowing that Alphonso would finish all three at the last possible minute.

Alphonso came home from a party, yawned, finished the paintings and went to bed.

Roderick, who was pretending to sleep, smiled to himself.

The three-pronged plan was in place.

The curtain was going up on disaster.

*           *           *           *

There was a big stink at the Modern Mid-Town Museum.

A small girl visiting the "Top Young Artists of New York" exhibit with her father noticed it first.

"Daddy, that picture stinks," she said in a loud voice.

"I don't agree at all," her father said, embarrassed. "I like the bright colors and the interesting detail."

"I don't mean *it isn't pretty,*" the little girl said. "I mean it *smells bad.*"

She stuck her nose within an inch of the painting.

"YECH, UGH, PHEW!" she yelled, holding her nose as her poor, embarrassed father dragged her from the museum.

Then adults began to notice.

"Percival, is it my imagination or is there an odd odor in here?" a woman asked her husband.

Percival sniffed. He frowned. He sniffed. He frowned.

"I believe you're right, Geraldine. I think it's coming from that heating duct," he said.

"Really?" Geraldine asked. "I thought it was coming from the corner by the window."

Actually, the odor seemed to be coming from everywhere.

Percival and Geraldine reported it to a guard, who called maintenance, who sent a janitor upstairs to investigate.

The janitor took three steps into the room before the odor hit him, but when it hit, it hit hard.

"Holy Toledo!" he groaned. "Where's it coming from?"

"Everywhere," the guard said.

"Smells like a sewer," the janitor said.

"Smells like rotten eggs," the guard said.

And, of course, he was right. It was rotten eggs — one of the world's most unpopular smells.

They searched the room for some time before figuring

out the stench came from foul-smelling white packets taped to the back of all the paintings. All the paintings, that is, but Alphonso Bean's.

An entire maintenance crew wearing gas masks had to take down the paintings, remove and dispose of the rotten egg packets, scrub the backs of the paintings with disinfectant and fumigate the museum.

The museum director supervised, wearing a gas mask and gritting her teeth. It took a huge hunk of the museum budget to pay for the damages, her museum was the laughing stock of Manhattan, and she was ticked. *Very* ticked.

And whom did she blame?

Alphonso Bean, of course.

"Never again," she fumed through her gas mask. "Alphonso is FINISHED at my museum. I wouldn't hang his paintings in a gas-station rest room."

Wasn't Alphonso's *the only painting* without rotten eggs on the back?

Weren't the eggs sewn into pieces of Alphonso's own World War I fighter-pilot style, white silk scarf?

Wasn't Alphonso notorious for his practical jokes?

\*            \*            \*            \*

Meanwhile, uptown . . . Alphonso Bean and the skinny and elegant Fortunada Trifle had just sat down at the head table at Fortunada's glittering charity banquet and ball.

Harp music wafted through the candlelight as hundreds of guests murmured and laughed and sipped Perrier and reached for the salt and pepper shakers.

Harp music and sneezes wafted through the room as scores of pepper caps plopped into salads, raising mini-storms of pepper.

Poor Fortunada Trifle, looking up to see what the trouble was, dumped an entire shaker of pepper onto her $10,000 beaded, royal-blue designer gown.

Alphonso was in shock. Somebody was up to *his* old tricks. He looked across the room at hundreds of fashionable guests sneezing to harp music, and he made a serious blunder.

He laughed.

"YOU!" Fortunada Trifle screamed, jumping up and trying to shake rivulets of pepper from between the beads of her $10,000, royal-blue designer gown.

"YOU DID THIS!" she screamed, pointing at Alphonso. "YOU AND YOUR JUVENILE, CHILDISH, SELF-CENTERED, CONCEITED, PUFFED UP, PHONY, CHEAP PRACTICAL JOKES!

"GET OUT OF MY PARTY! GET OUT OF MY LIFE! GET OUT OF NEW YORK!"

He tried to tell her he hadn't done it, but she just threw her Perrier at him.

Wasn't he notorious for his practical jokes?

\* \* \* \*

The phone was already ringing the next morning at "Post la Trende" gallery as the owner unlocked the front door.

An irate Texan was on the line. He was the gallery's best customer, and he was steamed.

"That durned Bean you sold me has disappeared," he shouted. "The one I paid you all those thousands and thousands of dollars for. I hanged the durned thing on the wall, and it's gone."

"You mean the painting is gone?" the shocked gallery

31

owner gasped.

"No, no, NO!" the Texan yelled. "The PAINTING'S here. The PAINT'S gone."

It was the starch Roderick had added to Alphonso's paint, of course. It made the paint flake as it dried, something like disappearing ink. Only it was disappearing paint.

The gallery owner dropped the phone and ran to check his other two new Beans. Sure enough, one was already a blank canvas and the other was foggy and fading fast.

The gallery owner was not amused.

First, he calmed down the irate Texan by promising to send back his thousands and thousands of dollars.

Then he called Alphonso.

Naturally, he thought the disappearing paint was some publicity ploy of Alphonso's and he was madder than ten ticked-off Texans.

"Get down here and get this disappearing so-called art *OUT* of here and make *YOURSELF* disappear and *NEVER COME BACK!*"

Alphonso tried to explain that he hadn't done anything to the paint. Like everybody else, he'd expected it to last forever.

But the gallery owner hung up on him.

After all, wasn't Alphonso notorious for his practical jokes?

*    *    *    *

Well, with his career in shambles and everybody in town on his case, there was nothing for Alphonso to do but pack up his paints, brushes and turpentine and leave New York.

Roderick helped him pack, a strange little smile playing

on his lips. But Alphonso was too upset to notice the smile. Or rather, he noticed but was too upset to think about it. At the time.

But later, he remembered that strange little smile when he read in "The New York Times" that Roderick won the "Young Artist in New York" competition.

Then he read in "Art News" that Roderick's paintings were selling faster than frozen yogurt. And it occurred to him that Roderick had been the only person with access to his long, white, World War I fighter pilot-style silk scarf.

Then he talked to a paint supply owner about chemicals that could make paint fade as it dried.

And he figured out the whole thing.

And he stopped painting, he stopped sleeping, and he almost stopped eating, because only one thought burned in his brain . . . revenge.

He began to plan the murder of Roderick Blaine.

# 6

"More tea?" Victoria Charmain asked.

She stopped summarizing *Artist's Revenge* and went back to pouring tea. Back to reality . . . if you can call tea at the Mayfair "reality."

"Did he do it?" Angela asked. "Did Alphonso murder Roderick?"

"How did he do it?" I asked.

"I hope he didn't use flying bats like in your *Phantom Cliffs* book," Vannie said.

Victoria laughed. "Well, I don't know yet. I'm still puzzling that out. He used poisonous mushrooms in my original draft, but mushroom murders have been so overdone in mysteries in the meantime, don't you think?"

"Er, I guess so," I said, but the truth was I couldn't cite one case of murder by mushroom, fact or fiction, for all the tea at the Mayfair.

"What do you mean 'in the meantime'? " Supergranny asked. "How long have you been working on this book?"

"Since 1958," Victoria answered.

We gasped. I knew writing was hard work, but I didn't know it was *that* hard.

She grinned. "Not constantly, of course. Actually, I wrote the original story years ago and when the publisher rejected it, I just locked it in my steamer trunk and forgot about it.

"About three months ago I was cleaning out the trunk and there it was. I started reading it and couldn't stop until I found out how it ended. I'd forgotten, you see, after all those years.

"So I decided to do a total rewrite and send it to my agent, who has been on my case about a new manuscript.

"It was a pretty darned good yarn if I do say so myself — except for the silly poisonous mushrooms," she said. "Back in those days I'd never had anything published and I didn't do quite enough rewriting. I didn't even use my own name then; I used a pseudonym. I was so green I thought you had to."

She laughed. "I called myself 'Penelope Pickwith.' How do you like it?"

"Love it," Angela said. "I remember reading in 'People Magazine' last year that you used to call yourself Penelope Pickwith."

"Well, if this harassment doesn't stop I may have to change my name again. Or leave town. Or both," she said, frowning.

"You say the trouble started with a phone call a month ago?" Supergranny asked.

"Right," Victoria said. "And it's gone from bad to worse. Calls at odd hours. Mysterious letters. Once a copy of Roderick Blaine's daily schedule was wadded up and stuck in my mailbox. Once a postcard with only two words, 'Pep-

35

per Caper,' was slipped under the door.

"Sometimes two or three of the crazy phone calls a week. Always in the middle of the night. Always the same silly voice like his mouth is full of raisin bran."

"Does he always say, 'This is Alphonso Bean?' " Angela asked.

"Not since the first time," she answered. "Until this morning he always said, 'Don't publish *Artist's Revenge.*' "

"And this morning?" Supergranny asked.

"This morning was a little scary . . . because somehow he'd gotten into the house."

"YOUR house?" Supergranny asked.

"MY house," Victoria answered.

"How did you know?" Vannie asked.

She leaned across the table. "Because when he called at 2 a.m. today he had a new message," she whispered. She paused.

We leaned toward her.

" 'Walking stick,' " she whispered. " 'Check the walking stick.' "

"Walking stick?" Vannie asked, scrunching her nose.

Victoria nodded slowly. "Remember Olivia's walking stick that we use for messages?"

I remembered it all right. I'd held it in my hand that very morning.

"After he hung up, I pulled on my robe and pulled up my courage and inched downstairs, carrying a flashlight. I half expected to bump into Alphonso Bean with a mouthful of raisin bran at every step.

"I KNEW it was impossible. Fictional characters can't just spring to life — but it seemed a little *less* impossible in the dark of 2 a.m.

36

"The walking stick was in the umbrella stand as usual. I grabbed it and hightailed it back upstairs, three steps at a time.

"By then my hands were shaking so badly, I could hardly unscrew the Wrigley Building top. Finally I got it off, and the message fell onto my bed . . . *a message from Alphonso Bean.*"

       *              *              *              *

The message she showed us had been wrapped around an orange-topped locker key. It was a tiny painting of a skull and crossbones, except that instead of crossed bones, it had two crossed paintbrushes. And instead of a skull, it had a very unflattering picture of Victoria's head.

And circling the picture were two words: *Artist's Revenge.*

"The key was for a locker in the Art Institute checkroom and that was the 'mysterious errand' Olivia told you about.

"I stopped by your hotel to see if you'd go with me, but you weren't there."

"We were biking along the lake," I said.

"And at your house," Angela said.

"And with the frogs," Vannie said.

"Right," Victoria said. "So anyway, I just went over to the Art Institute by myself and got the package, then sat down by one of the lions out front to open it."

"Where is it?" Supergranny asked.

"I threw it away as fast as I could find a garbage can," she said. "It was rotten eggs. A whole stinking package of rotten eggs."

# 7

Supergranny was *not* going to let the Charmains spend another night alone in that house.

Not after she heard about Alphonso getting *inside* the house.

*We* would move in with them. *We* would protect them. From an imaginary guy in a mystery novel. An imaginary guy in a mystery novel no one had ever read.

Unfortunately, we had to move in behind Olivia's back. Victoria was so worried about too much stress for Olivia that she didn't want her to hear a peep about Alphonso. That's why she hadn't called the police or had a tracer put on her telephone.

We hung around our Barclay suite playing gin rummy, eating room-service pizza and reviewing the case:

- Victoria wrote *Artist's Revenge* in 1958.
- After the publisher rejected it, she locked it in her trunk, and forgot it.
- Three months ago, she started rewriting it.
- The trouble started the night of her Mayhem Mystery

Writers Club one month ago with a mysterious phone call from a guy claiming to be Alphonso Bean.

"So, even though she never showed the book to a soul, someone found out all about it, and is trying to stop its publication," Angela said.

". . . Or Alphonso Bean has come to life," Vannie added.

Just then, Victoria called to tell us Olivia was asleep and the coast was clear.

We went downstairs, and the doorman flagged us a cab. We were going to sleep in our sweats and sneak back to the Barclay early in the morning before Olivia woke up.

At least that was the plan, but Shackleford and Chesterton threw a monkey wrench into it by barking and beeping their heads off as soon as our cab pulled up to Charmain's row house.

They were so excited about the chance of another root-beer barrel windfall, they couldn't control themselves. They made enough racket to wake greater Chicago.

"Would you please stifle it before we get arrested?" I told Shackleford when I saw someone in the next row house pulling back a curtain to watch us.

Victoria let us in before we got hauled to jail for disturbing the peace, and we settled down in the gallery in sleeping bags and old quilts she'd rounded up.

Sleeping on an art gallery floor rolled up in a patchwork quilt is no suite at the Barclay, but I tried to make the best of it.

Old hairy Shackleford settled down beside me, and Chesterton scooted between Angela and Vannie and switched off his lights and beeper.

Before you could say "skull and crossbrushes" everybody

was asleep. Everybody but me. It was too dark to see anybody, but I could hear Supergranny's even breathing from the couch.

Angela, Vannie and Chesterton slept happily under the gargantuan rubber plant in the bay window.

I was closest to the hall.

Through the archway, I could barely see the shadowy staircase. A patch of light from a streetlight crept through the front door glass, falling on the walking stick in the umbrella stand.

Its gold Wrigley Building gleamed like a prop on a dark stage.

It was after midnight, and the house was still.

I turned my head so I couldn't see the dumb walking stick.

Unfortunately, I could still see it in my mind. In my mind, the front door opened. A figure reached for the walking stick. He unscrewed the top . . .

I turned back for a quick look at the walking stick to be sure nobody was there.

Nobody was there.

The walking stick just sat there in the umbrella stand, its gold Wrigley Building gleaming in the streetlight.

What, exactly, was I supposed to do if a murderer in a book turned into a real guy and landed in that hall?

And how had his message gotten into the walking stick last night?

A terrible thought barged into my head: *Was there another message in the walking stick?*

Could someone have slipped in a message when we weren't looking? Beamed in a message?

How did we know it wasn't some kind of hi-tech walking stick?

Maybe it received satellite messages through the air.

Maybe it worked like some kind of fax machine you don't have to plug in.

Maybe I was going bonkers.

Another terrible thought barged into my head: *I had to have a look inside that walking stick.*

Oh no, you don't, I told myself. You're not going to get up in the dark and walk into that hall and open that walking stick.

*But I had to have a look inside that walking stick.*

I wished somebody would wake up. I poked Shackleford, but she just snorted, smacked her lips and rolled over.

I sat up in my quilt. *Oh no you don't,* I told myself. *This is as far as you go.*

I stood up.

What was that? I thought I'd heard a noise. I sort of half-stood, half-sat, wrapped in my quilt like a mummy. A mummy in a house as quiet as a mummy's tomb.

I inched across the floor to the hallway and stopped to listen. Nothing. Mummy quiet.

I grabbed the walking stick and held it up in the light from the door. Hanging onto my quilt with one hand, I tried to unscrew the top with the other. Finally I got the Wrigley Building off and shook the stick. Nothing fell out. I held it up and peered inside.

Suddenly there was a noise on the stairs behind me. I whirled around just as a shadowy figure grabbed me.

\*      \*      \*      \*

Blazing lights and screams filled the hall.

A gray robe and wild gray hair swooped around me as one bony hand grabbed my sleeve and another snatched the walking stick from my grasp.

It was Olivia Charmain.

I don't know which of us was more surprised.

She stopped screaming and froze in place, holding the walking stick over my head. Her gray robe and wild gray hair settled around her. I stopped screaming and stared.

There we stood, still as wax.

"Joshua?" she gasped.

"I can explain," I gasped back.

Supergranny, Angela, Vannie, Shackleford and Chesterton swarmed around us as Victoria clattered down the stairs.

"Victoria, you're behind this," Olivia said, still staring at me, still clutching my sleeve in her bony fingers, still holding the walking stick above my head.

Nothing moved but her lips, and nothing of mine moved at all. Why move and maybe set off that screaming again? And that long, swirling robe? That wild gray hair?

*"What is going ONNNN, Victoria???"* Olivia hissed through clenched teeth.

I stared at her clenched teeth and knew it had been a mistake not to level with her from the start. Olivia is NOT the kind of woman you want to make mad if you have a choice.

All things considered, I'd rather have been at the Barclay.

Somehow the others pried the walking stick from her fist, moved us into the living room and poured tea.

I rewrapped myself in my quilt and sat down against the fireplace. Shackleford and Vannie and Angela sat around me.

I knew they could tell I was still terrified by the way my teeth chattered, but who cared? I'm not proud. I was plenty glad to have a few bodies around for Olivia to trip over in case she lunged for me again.

But she didn't.

In fact, after we apologized for sneaking into her house, she kept pushing root-beer barrels at me to try to make up. I'm not crazy about root-beer barrels at 1 a.m., but she meant it as a peace offering, so I did my best. She said a noise out front had awakened her (probably Shackleford and Chesterton). Then as she was dozing off again, she'd heard me moving downstairs.

We finally got Victoria to tell her the whole story. It didn't seem to stress out Olivia at all. If anything, she enjoyed it.

Victoria finished the summary of *Artist's Revenge* about 2 a.m. Somewhere along the way my teeth stopped chattering and I started to nod off. *Artist's Revenge* isn't exactly a peaceful bedtime story, but it was the second time I'd heard it and I'd had a rough day.

I was just dozing off when Olivia dropped the bomb.

"Oh yes, I remember that," she said. "It happened so long ago I'd forgotten."

Victoria looked puzzled. "What do you mean, 'it happened'?" she asked. "I never showed you my manuscript."

"No, no, not your manuscript," Olivia said. "The actual event you based the story on."

"It WASN'T an actual event," Victoria said, annoyed. "I made it up. It's total fiction."

Olivia cocked an eyebrow. "Victoria, darling, I hate to differ, but I remember the whole thing. It was right before I left New York to open my Paris gallery. The papers were full of it: the stink at the Modern Museum, the pepper

43

shaker problem at the charity ball, the young artist slinking out of New York in disgrace.

"Of course his name wasn't Alphonso Bean. It was Arklett, Arkbuckle, Arkbutt . . . Arksomething or other, I can't remember."

"Olivia, dear, you're wrong. I MADE IT UP," Victoria said, every word slow and distinct like she was GET-TING VERY ANGRY.

"Victoria, dear, I don't know why you're offended. Mystery writers often ARE IN-SPIRED BY REAL CRIMES," Olivia said, dripping sweetness like she was also GET-TING VERY ANGRY.

The whole thing was GET-TING VERY TENSE. They were starting to sound like Angela, Vannie and me. A sibling fight at their age! They were past 50! Waaay past 50! It was embarrassing.

"I made it up!" Victoria shouted.

"You didn't!" Olivia shouted.

"I did!"

"You didn't!"

"I did!"

"You didn't!"

"HOLD IT!" Supergranny thundered, jumping to her feet and spreading her arms like an umpire at home plate. "HOLDITHOLDITHOLDITHOLDIT!"

They held it.

"Now. Olivia," Supergranny said, returning to the couch and taking a sip of tea. "Do you remember when all this happened?"

"Of course, I remember," Olivia said airily. "Because I remember where I was when I read about it in 'The New York Times'.

"I was standing on the deck of the Queen Elizabeth II the day I sailed for France. And I remember it was Election Day because I stopped at the polls to vote on my way to the dock.

"It was the day John F. Kennedy was elected president of the United States in November, 1960."

"There, you see, my book was first!" Victoria said grandly. "I finished it in 1959 and by Election Day it had been locked in my trunk for almost a year. I told you I didn't base the book on a real event!"

"No, but the events may be based on your book," Supergranny said slowly.

"Someone may have read your manuscript and used your ideas to destroy a rival," Angela said excitedly.

"And now he's afraid the world will find out," I said.

"So he wants to stop your book," Vannie added.

"But who?" Victoria said. "And how did he find out I planned to publish it after all these years?"

At that, a strange look came across Olivia's face, but nobody seemed to notice but me. She looked as if she'd remembered something. She cleared her throat and I thought she was going to tell us what it was, but she didn't.

I should have asked. Maybe she wouldn't have told us, but I should have asked. Oh, how I wish I'd asked.

Operation "Find Arkbutt" began at dawn.

"He's key," Supergranny said.

"If he can lead us to the crook who torpedoed his career, we'll find Victoria's villain. I'd bet my southeast corner on it."

You may already know about Supergranny's southeast corner in her workshop-office-laboratory-playroom-garage. In my opinion, her workshop-office-laboratory-playroom-garage is the best room in the world. You could look for 137 years and not find a better one.

I first saw it the day we moved from Cleveland, and it was quite a shock.

I was at her house hunting Shackleford, who had lost herself, when I stumbled across Supergranny's secret office behind her fireplace. You just eat a snickerdoodle cookie with the secret ingredient, push a yellow button by the fireplace, and — whammo! — the fireplace springs open and "Stars and Stripes Forever" booms out of the ceiling.

It's where she keeps Chesterton, the Ferrari, and of course her southeast corner, with the basketball court, costume room, swimming pool, and on and on. She says everybody needs a room like that and maybe by the time I'm her age everybody will have one.

I hope she's right. I really hope she's right.

Anyway, her office is also where she keeps her microfilm, which is what we needed for Operation Find Arkbutt.

"Fat lot of good my microfilm equipment is doing us sitting 160 miles away at home," she grumbled as we left the Barclay after stopping to change clothes that morning. "But you just can't pack everything. Thank heaven for the Chicago Public Library. Its microfilm files are as good as mine. Maybe better."

We were at the library before the doors opened, our pockets weighted down with change to pay for copies of any 1960 "New York Times" story about Arkbutt we could find.

"Of course his name might not BE Arkbutt," Angela pointed out. "Olivia called him 'Arklett, Arkbuckle, Arkbutt or Arksomething or other.'"

"Yeah, but we can call him Arkbutt until we find out his real name," I said. "I like the sound of it."

"Me, too." Vannie said.

We checked out the reel of microfilm for "The New York Times," Nov. 1-10, 1960, and Angela slipped it onto the spindle and flicked on the machine.

"Joshua, do the honors," Supergranny said, meaning I could advance the microfilm first. I sat down in front of the viewer and turned the crank forward. Pages of "The New York Times" whipped by on the screen, too fast to read. It reminded me of driving a ski boat, and all the stories skimming by made me dizzy.

Not enough sleep and too many root-beer barrels the night before had made me slightly seasick anyway.

Vannie took over when we got to November 5th, turning the film more slowly so she wouldn't sail right past Tuesday, November 8, which had been Election Day.

She sailed past the first section anyway and was already to sports before she could stop. She backed up to Page 1 with so many jerky stops and starts I thought I'd have to go wait outside until my stomach settled.

But I just kept swallowing, and after we waded through what seemed about a million stories on the Richard Nixon-John Kennedy election and actress Brigitte Bardot's new film and everything else that happened on Nov. 8, 1960, we finally found it.

It was a story about a young artist who had to leave New York in disgrace after he was blamed for a chain of sicko practical jokes. The story didn't actually say he was guilty, but it didn't actually say he wasn't either.

"And it sure doesn't say where he went," Angela said.

"Or where he was from," Vannie said.

"But it does give his name," Supergranny said.

We had to laugh. His name wasn't Arkbutt, but we could see where Olivia had gotten it.

"Olivia remembered his name had something to do with 'Ark,' " Angela said. "She must have been thinking of 'Noah's Ark.' Not bad after all these years."

His name was Noah Z. Barklett.

*          *          *          *

"At last — a good lead!" Supergranny said.

"The name of a man who left New York City in 1960?" Angela asked.

"That's a good lead?" Vannie asked.

Supergranny laughed. "What did you expect? A note at the bottom of the story saying, 'Thirty years from now, Mr. Barklett will be . . .' with an address and phone number?"

"It would help," I said.

"True," she said with a grin. "But it didn't, so we spring immediately into Operation Find Barklett. Meet me at 'Out-of-Town Telephone Books' in three minutes."

She tossed yellow highlighters from her purse to Vannie and me, told us to mark any clues to finding Barklett and took off.

Angela made four copies of the story, then rewound the microfilm and gave it to Vannie to turn in at the desk.

I highlighted every possible clue on my copy of the story.

I got six:

1. Noah Z. Barklett.

2. Charlene Zimbwit. (She wrote the story.)

3. Galleria Soho (where Barklett's pictures had faded just like Alphonso Bean's at "Post la Trende" in the book).

4. Susanna Delmontwinkle (whose charity banquet had been wrecked by pepper just like Fortunada Trifle's in the book).

5. Avant-Garde Museum (where there'd been a rotten egg stink just like at the Modern Mid-Town Museum in the book).

6. "The New York Times."

Vannie highlighted the same words on the other three copies of the story.

In three minutes we regrouped by the telephone books, where Supergranny had just plopped the fat Manhattan White Pages and even fatter Manhattan Yellow Pages on a table.

"Check 'Noah Z. Barklett' first," she said, pushing the White Pages toward me. "Who knows? Maybe he moved back to New York."

"Strike 1," I said. If Barklett was back in New York, he didn't have a phone. Or wasn't listed. Anyway, he wasn't there.

"Check 'Charlene Zimbwit,' " Supergranny said. "She wrote the story. Maybe she remembers where he went."

"Strike 2," Vannie said. There wasn't any Charlene Zimbwit listed. Maybe she had married and changed her name. Maybe she had divorced and changed her name. Maybe she had moved. Anyway, she wasn't there.

"Check Galleria Soho," Supergranny said.

"Strike 3," Angela said. The Galleria Soho had either closed or changed its name because it wasn't listed under "Galleria" or "Soho" in the White Pages or under "art galleries" in the Yellow Pages.

"New batter," Supergranny said. "Check Susanna Delmontwinkle, Avant-Garde Museum and 'The New York Times.' "

"Base hit," I said. "There are a zillion Delmontwinkles." I plopped the phone book upside down on the copying machine, Vannie dropped in a quarter and we copied the whole page of Delmontwinkles.

"Rounding second," Angela said. "There are three numbers for the Avant-Garde Museum." She wrote them on her copy of the story.

"Third base," Vannie said. " 'The New York Times' has a whole string of numbers."

"Nice work," Supergranny said. She slammed the telephone books shut. "Get ready to steal home."

# 9

We moved on to the Chicago Art Institute and set up shop on the bench nearest "Paris, A Rainy Day."

You'll remember that "Paris, A Rainy Day" is a "regular" on Supergranny's Hit List. That means she'll visit it or bust on every trip to Chicago, including this one.

"Who says we can't mix pleasure with business?" she asked.

The business was "Operation Find Noah Barklett" (formerly "Find Arkbutt"). But we'll get to that in a minute.

First, the pleasure — "Paris, A Rainy Day," a giant oil painting. Its real name is "The Place de l'Europe on a Rainy Day," and it was painted by a rich French engineer named Gustave Caillebotte in 1877.

"WELL?" Supergranny asked.

We knew what the "Well?" meant.

It meant she expected us to brag about the painting and brag hard.

She's like that with anything she considers first-class. She expects it to get sincere and serious praise — dumptrucks

51

and avalanches of praise.

No way could we get away with saying "too many dull grays for me" or "too much like a photograph" or even "very interesting."

"WELLLL?" she asked again.

Vannie started. "I like that you can smell the rain."

She was right. Something about the way the rain in the painting glistened on the sidewalk and collected between cobblestones made you swear you could smell fresh, clean rain.

"I like that it's big," I said. It was bigger than the world map in my class at school, which is just big enough in my opinion. I hate dinky paintings.

"I like the old-fashioned clothes," Angela said. "And the way the woman's long skirt sweeps to her left as she walks and the man's high-topped hat and all the matching umbrellas and the way everybody has someplace interesting to go but nobody is in too much of a hurry." She stopped for breath.

Supergranny just sat there, waiting for more.

Angela took a deep breath and forged ahead. "I like that the painting makes me feel calm without making me feel bored."

That ought to do it, I thought, sneaking a sideways glance at Supergranny.

No such luck. She just sat there, waiting.

Angela frowned at me behind Supergranny's back and jerked her head toward the painting, urging me to take over the praise. I knew we were stuck there until we came up with something, but I couldn't think of zip.

I frowned at Vannie and jerked MY head at the painting, hoping she'd have better luck.

"I like how . . ." Vannie paused, chewing her index fingernail.

Angela and I both frowned at her and kept jerking our heads at the painting, urging her to get on with it.

"How . . . you can look way down three different streets in the back of the painting, down through the mist and rain and still see people going places and doing things."

That got us off the hook.

"Yes. Great." Supergranny said, jumping up. "I thought you'd like it. Now we've got to get back to work."

She fished her telephone credit card out of her purse.

"To the phones!"

*       *       *       *

We grabbed side-by-side phones in the basement of the Art Institute and Supergranny gave us a quick "How To Make Long Distance Calls With A Telephone Credit Card" refresher course.

Phone Team One — Angela and I — started calling the Delmontwinkle list we'd copied at the library.

Phone Team Two — Supergranny and Vannie — started calling the Avant-Garde Museum and "The New York Times".

We were trying to come up with somebody — anybody — who could help us find Noah Z. Barklett.

Angela and I took turns. She got a busy signal and a no answer before she finally connected.

"Hello, this is Angela Poindexter calling from the Chicago Art Institute," she said politely, reading from the speech Supergranny had written down. "I'm trying to reach a Ms. Susanna Delmontwinkle. Could you tell me if I have the right Delmontwinkle residence?"

It wasn't, so she went on to the next question Super-granny had written: "Do you happen to know where I could locate Susanna Delmontwinkle, who lived in New York in 1960?"

The idea was to reach a Delmontwinkle cousin or aunt or somebody who could steer us to the right Susanna Delmontwinkle, the woman whose charity banquet had been wrecked by pepper just like Fortunada Trifle's in Victoria's book.

I thought we'd hit pay dirt because the person in New York kept jabbering and Angela kept nodding and saying, "Oh, really?"

"Write it down," I hissed.

She just turned her back on me and went on saying "Oh, really?" Finally she hung up and groaned.

"What did he say?" I asked.

"It was a she and the only other Delmontwinkles she knew were Sally, Roxanne and Ralph, and she hasn't spoken to Ralph since she divorced him in 1978 and Sally and Roxanne have moved to Montana where, according to the last report she had, Sally was selling Amway and Roxanne was working as a ranch house cook and, at any rate, neither of them was even born in 1960 with the possible exception of Roxanne who has been known to lie about her age, but even so, would have been a baby in 1960 — do you want the rest?"

"No," I said, trading places with her.

I dialed my first Delmontwinkle. After nine rings I was about to hang up when I got a VERY angry and wet Charles Delmontwinkle on the phone.

He'd been in the shower and wasn't a bit happy to be out. And, no, he "sure as X**#@# didn't know any

Susanna Delmontwinkle." I hung up with my ears ringing. I'd never been sworn at long-distance before.

"At least it was short," Angela said.

We took a break to check with Supergranny and Vannie in the next booth.

Supergranny had an editor at "The New York Times" on the line. "He says Charlene Zimbwit has retired and is living in Connecticut," Vannie whispered. "He's giving Supergranny her number."

Hooray! Zimbwit, you remember, was the reporter who wrote the story on Barklett in 1960.

"We're not to home plate yet," Supergranny said, hanging up. "Get back to the Delmontwinkles."

We went back to our booth and Angela dialed N.S. Delmontwinkle.

BINGO!

"It IS?" she asked, getting so excited she dropped her pen on the floor.

"You're THE Susanna Delmontwinkle who lived in New York in 1960?" she said, motioning frantically for me to pick up the pen, which I frantically tried to do while she stepped all over my fingers.

Finally she finished writing everything Susanna Delmontwinkle told her, thanked her 412 times and hung up.

"JOSHUA, YOU'RE NOT GOING TO BELIEVE THIS!" she yelled, as Supergranny and Vannie crowded around our booth.

"HE'S HERE!" Supergranny and Angela yelled together.

"NOAH BARKLETT IS LIVING IN CHICAGO AND WORKING AT THE 'CHICAGO TRIBUNE'!"

## 10

The Billy Goat Tavern is under Michigan Avenue.

That's right. Under. Down a staircase in the sidewalk by the REAL Wrigley Building.

The real Wrigley is exactly like the little one on Olivia's walking stick, except that instead of being gold it's creamy white and looks like a humongous wedding cake.

"This can't be right," you think when you get to the bottom of the staircase. "This is some kind of giant parking garage. Where's the Billy Goat?"

Then you realize the corner you just turned IS the Billy Goat, or at least part of its outside wall.

We were meeting Noah Z. Barklett.

At first when Supergranny called him at the "Tribune", he'd refused to meet us.

"But it's urgent," she told him.

"No," he said.

And could you blame him?

Here we were, four downstaters he didn't know from Al Capone, and she wouldn't even TRY to explain why we wanted to see him.

But could you blame her?

You can't just call a total stranger and say that in 1960 an unpublished book gave SOMEONE the idea to demolish his career and he had to help find that SOMEONE to stop another crime.

Face it. It sounds loony.

So Supergranny stooped to name-dropping.

"We're friends of Victoria Charmain," she said.

That softened him up a little. He's a big Charmain fan.

Then she stooped to bribery.

"We'll buy you a cheeseburger at the Billy Goat," she said.

That did it.

He agreed to meet us after work, giving us just enough time to see five thousand more paintings and statues at the Art Institute plus enough fancy dishes and jewelry boxes to last a lifetime.

We pushed through the red door and down the steps into the smoky, noisy, crowded tavern and crossed through a long line of people waiting to buy cheeseburgers and stuff.

We found a little red-checked table and sat down to wait for Barklett.

The room was lined with framed news stories about the Billy Goat and pictures of Chicago political bosses, sports greats, newspeople, actors and other famous and notorious people.

Nobody was very dressed up, unless you count the guy dressed like a musketeer and carrying a sword.

"I bet that's Barklett," Angela whispered.

But it wasn't. He just stared at us a minute, then went back to staring at the woman he was with.

"How are we going to find him?" I asked.

"Relax; he'll find us," Supergranny said. "I described us over the phone, and nobody else here looks like us."

For sure.

As far as I could see, we were the only table with a gray-haired woman and three kids, so we stood out. Not as much as if we'd brought Shackleford and Chesterton, but still, we stood out.

After about five minutes, a guy from the other side of the room picked up his drink and moseyed our way. He had wiry gray hair and was on the pudgy side.

"He doesn't LOOK like Alphonso Bean," Vannie whispered.

"Of course not," Angela said out of the side of her mouth. "Alphonso Bean is fiction."

With a jolt I realized I'd expected Barklett to look like Alphonso, too — complete with tuxedo jacket, jeans, sandals and a long, white, World War I fighter pilot-style scarf.

But, of course, he wouldn't. Alphonso was a character in a book. Barklett was real. The only connection between them was SOMEONE had used the ideas in the book to ruin Barklett's career, the way Roderick had ruined Alphonso's.

"Ms. Oglepop?" he asked, holding out his hand.

"Mr. Barklett, how kind of you to meet us," Supergranny said. "Won't you sit down. I have a very strange story to tell you."

She sent Angela, Vannie and me off to the line to buy cheeseburgers and fries while she explained the whole, rotten scheme.

*     *     *     *

Everything had happened pretty much as we'd figured.

"It was so long ago . . . I've forgotten the details," Barklett was saying as we got back to the table with the cheeseburgers.

"I was young and having a blast in New York. But when I took the rap for those raunchy practical jokes, I figured it was time to say, 'Goodbye, Big Apple; Hellooo, Windy City!'

"I got a job in display advertising at the 'Sun-Times', moved to the 'Tribune' and was promoted to supervisor. I met my wife, who was working in classified, and after the four kids came along I gradually stopped painting. To tell you the truth, I didn't miss it much. I guess I've been happy without it.

"And in all these years I never realized those jokes were a plot to get ME. I thought I'd just had the bad luck to catch the blame." He laughed. "Not that I hadn't ESCAPED the blame for a few jokes I DESERVED being run out of town for.

"But I can't believe that someone is trying to stop Victoria Charmain's new book because of ME. Are you sure?"

"Affirmative," Supergranny said.

"He's probably afraid you'll read the book, realize he zonked you in 1960 and sue him," Angela said.

"Or murder him, like Alphonso does in the book," Vannie said.

Barklett choked on his cheeseburger. "Murder's out, Vannie," he said. "Not my style at all."

We were all relieved to hear it. He did seem MUCH more reasonable than Alphonso.

"But who could have done it?" Supergranny asked.

"Who could have known about Victoria's book?" Angela

asked.

"Who was jealous of you?" I asked.

"Who was mean enough to stir disappearing goop in your paint?" Vannie asked.

He looked thoughtful. He frowned. He finished his cheeseburger. He ate the rest of Vannie's fries.

Then he leaned back, crossed his legs and said, "I'm sorry, I can't help you. It's preposterous.

"The only person I know who might have read that book was my roommate. He picked up extra money working as a free-lance reader for a publisher. He read manuscripts and told the editor whether he thought books should be published."

"So he COULD have read Victoria's manuscript?" Angela asked.

"I suppose it's possible," Barklett said.

"His name?" Supergranny asked.

Barklett frowned again. He ate the rest of my fries.

"But he's a very successful artist," he said. "When he moved to Chicago about eight months ago, I helped get a story about him in the 'Tribune'."

"His name?" Supergranny asked.

"He couldn't have . . ." Barklett said.

"His NAME?" Supergranny asked.

"Lionel," Barklett whispered.

"LIONEL!" Sirens shrieked in my brain. Lionel was the artist who had done the paintings of Olivia Charmain! The one in the hall with her head on the rocking chair! The one above the mantle with the staircase behind her.

"He's here," Barklett whispered.

"Here in Chicago?" Supergranny asked.

"No. I mean yes. I mean HERE at the Billy Goat. He

came in about the time you did. I was talking with him before I came over to your table."

He nodded toward the bar.

Four of us spun around and stared at the bar.

A man was dashing for the exit.

"THE POISON-FROG MAN!" Vannie yelled.

"THE MAN WHO HAS BEEN FOLLOWING US!" Angela yelled.

"AFTER HIM!" Supergranny yelled.

Supergranny crashed through the cheeseburger line and out the Billy Goat door.

Angela, Vannie, Barklett and I burst outside after her.

A million cars rumbled on the roads overhead, but here all seemed quiet and deserted in the streetlight shadows. A dirty breeze swirled old paper cups and potato-chip bags around our ankles. A lone cab passed in the distance.

At first I thought Lionel might be lurking behind one of the thick, steel girders holding up the roads above. But in the same instant we glimpsed him disappearing up the Michigan Avenue stairs.

We raced for the stairs and clattered after him.

"SCRAM SEVEN!" Supergranny yelled at the top.

Scram Seven is a chase code. It means:

1. Break into two teams.
2. Team one — left!
3. Team two — right!
4. If you don't spot the target, report back to start in five minutes.
5. If you DO spot the target, signal.

(Supergranny uses several signals: Tarzan yells, whistles, Shackleford barks, semaphores, her red, white and blue Gucci scarf, and flares. Scram Seven calls for the Tarzan yell.)

Team One (Supergranny and Vannie) turned left and dashed up Michigan Avenue. Team Two (Angela and I) dashed right.

Nobody had time to assign Barklett a team, so he just galloped after Angela and me, which was fine with us. We could use all the help we could get if we caught Lionel.

But catching him was a long shot.

Night had arrived while we were at the Billy Goat, making it tough enough to spot him. But, worse, even more people were rushing up and down Michigan Avenue.

Try as we might to dodge between groups, we were slowed almost to a crawl as we crossed the Chicago River bridge. We ran south for a good five minutes without a single glimpse of him, then collapsed against a trash can to catch our breath.

I was a little worried about Barklett because he was gasping and his face was purple. He was either out of shape or the truth about his old friend was too much for him.

"I still can't — gasp — believe it," he said. "I've never seen Lionel disembark the Billy Goat THAT fast.

"He SURE — gasp — ACTED guilty," he continued between great gasps and exhales. "Don't you think he ACTED guilty?"

"Well, you're innocent until PROVEN guilty in this country, of course," Angela answered, "but he ACTED guilty as sin."

We waited until Barklett stopped gasping and his face wasn't so purple, then headed back toward the Wrigley Building. Its spotlights had come on and it gleamed in their light like the moon reflecting sunlight.

Angela insisted we stop on the bridge to enjoy it, which

was all right with Barklett, who was ready for another rest.

Supergranny and Vannie joined us and leaned against the railing.

"Nichts," Supergranny said, German for "nothing," meaning they hadn't seen hide or hair of Lionel either. We'd lost him.

Barklett didn't even have his address or phone number.

"He moved a month ago and never gave me his address," he said. "And his phone number has always been unlisted."

"Family? Girlfriend? Anyone who might know where to find him?" Supergranny asked.

Barklett shook his head and looked miserable. "Not as far as I know. He's always been a loner.

"He sure ACTED guilty, didn't he?" he asked again, staring across the water at the Wrigley Building.

"Guilty as sin," Angela agreed.

        \*            \*            \*           \*

We thanked Barklett for his help and put him in a cab for home.

"Our only hope is Olivia," Supergranny said as we stood on the curb trying to flag another cab for ourselves. "Since she hangs Lionel's paintings in her gallery, surely she knows where he lives."

"You don't suppose . . .?" Angela said.

"Suppose what, dear?" Supergranny asked, scowling at an empty cab that whipped right past us.

"You don't think it's possible . . .?" Angela asked.

"Think what's possible?" Supergranny asked, then gave a shrill whistle between her fingers at another cab.

"Never mind," Angela said as the cab skidded to a stop

and we climbed inside.

I hate it when she does that.

"Out with it, Angela," I said crossly. "Outwithitoutwithit-outwithit."

"Wellllll . . . you don't suppose Olivia is in cahoots with Lionel, do you?" she asked quietly, so the cab driver couldn't hear.

"But why would she help someone stop her own sister's book?" Vannie asked.

Angela shrugged and frowned. "I don't know. Jealousy? Money? To protect Victoria somehow? Like if she secretly read the book and thought it stank and didn't want it to ruin Victoria's reputation as a writer?"

"Nooooo, I don't think so, honey," Supergranny said. "Despite the Charmains' fusses, they're devoted to each other. Olivia would cut off her foot to help Victoria. But she MAY have been duped into helping Lionel without knowing it. . . . Like that note in the walking stick, for instance."

I'd been thinking the same thing. "Yeah, because Olivia knew Lionel, she might have told him about using the walking stick for messages."

"Right," Angela said. "And he might have dropped by for a visit and while she was fixing tea or getting more root-beer barrels —"

"Clunk! — he drops the message in the walking stick for Victoria to find after he calls at 2 a.m.!" Vannie said.

"It fits," Supergranny agreed. "That much of it."

"One time last night," I said. "After Olivia caught me with the walking stick and tried to kill me —"

"Don't exaggerate," Angela said.

I ignored her. "— she acted like she was going to tell

us something. She cleared her throat and opened her mouth — but that was as far as she got."

"Do you suppose she started to suspect Lionel?" Angela asked.

"She wouldn't be silly enough to ASK him about it . . . would she?" I asked slowly.

It got very quiet in the cab. Nobody said anything for two blocks. Everybody was thinking the same thing: She might. She just might.

Finally, Supergranny broke the silence. "I could just kick myself for letting Lionel follow us straight to the Billy Goat. He must have been tailing us all day. As soon as he saw us with Barklett, he knew we were on to him."

"So now, he may be desperate . . ." Angela said slowly.

"And he might go after Olivia — or the others," Supergranny said. She glanced at her watch. "We're due to meet Victoria, Olivia, Shackleford and Chesterton at the Mayhem Mystery Writers Club in five minutes. I just hope Lionel doesn't get to them first."

She leaned toward the driver and slipped him a five.

"If you know any shortcuts, we'd appreciate it. The friends we're meeting may be in serious trouble."

"Very serious trouble," she repeated softly, staring out the window at the dazzling lights of Michigan Avenue.

# 11

The Mayhem Mystery Writers meet in a secret room above Polly's Supper Club in the Loop.

It was raining when we climbed out of the cab and crossed the street under the thundering El. Neon signs blinked all around us and shimmered from every puddle and window.

Polly's was packed.

It's the kind of low-ceilinged, maroon and black room that feels like a basement, even though it's not. The waiters wear tuxedos and the customers wear just about everything else: sports jackets, windbreakers, shirtsleeves, bomber jackets, brownish-purple dresses with fringe — just about everything else.

"Holmes," Supergranny whispered to Fred, the headwaiter.

We knew he was Fred because Victoria had described him when she gave us the passwords to get into the Mayhem Mystery Writers' monthly meeting.

"You mean Oliver Wendell?" Fred asked.

That's what he was supposed to ask — did we mean the late, great Supreme Court Justice Oliver Wendell Holmes?

We all shook our heads.

"Sherlock," Vannie whispered.

That's what we were supposed to answer — that we meant the famous detective Sherlock Holmes.

Fred nodded. "Follow me," he said.

We followed him to the back of the room and past the rest-room sign into a hallway with three doors marked "Men," "Women," and "Closet."

Fred opened the closet door, except it wasn't a closet. It was a steep staircase with a purple door at the top. He motioned us up the stairs and returned to his headwaitering.

"Hurry," Supergranny said. We rumbled up the stairs and crowded around the purple door.

It sounded like a convention inside. A noisy convention.

. I knocked three times. Nothing happened.

"Knock again, Joshua," Supergranny said. "I wish they'd hurry. Heaven knows what Lionel is up to."

I knocked three more times. Nothing.

"Oh, for Pete's sake. They're partying so hard they can't hear their own door. POUND it, Joshua," Supergranny ordered.

I really let the door have it. Three times.

A peephole cover slid back. An eye stared out at us.

"CHRISTIE!" Angela shouted the upstairs password.

"CHRISTIE BRINKLEY?" The eye's voice shouted back.

That's what it was supposed to ask: Did we mean famous model Christie Brinkley?

"AGATHA!" we shouted.

That's what we were supposed to answer — that we meant famous mystery writer Agatha Christie.

The peephole slammed shut. A bolt slid open. Another bolt slid open. The door opened.

"Welcome to the Mayhem Mystery Writers' monthly meeting," said a woman in a flowered dress and huge hat.

*       *       *       *

A long table with high-backed leather chairs stood absolutely empty in the center of the room.

Half the mystery writers were gathered in a corner, holding glasses in one hand and toothpicks in the other. They were waving the toothpicks in the air while they shouted at a bearded man holding a small robot.

The bearded man was popping peanuts into the sensor on the robot's head. Every time he popped in a peanut, the robot went "Cling, cling" and flashed his green blinker and all the mystery writers laughed and yelled, "Give him another peanut!"

Meanwhile, the other half of the mystery writers were in another corner, cheering on a woman in silver dangle earrings who was throwing tiny meatballs at a large hairy dog.

Everytime she threw a meatball, the dog jumped into the air for it, missed, then skidded across the floor after it and gobbled it down.

The mystery writers were laughing as if this was the funniest thing they'd ever seen or heard.

"Throw her a stuffed mushroom!" yelled a mystery writer in the crowd. "Throw her a fried cauliflower," yelled another. "She likes the fried cauliflower."

It was disgusting. And it was not the slightest bit funny to anyone who'd ever nursed Shackleford through diarrhea. Or seen Chesterton with his circuits shorted out.

Supergranny was ticked. She pulled her tornado siren whistle out of her purse and blew.

Fifty mystery writers froze in place.

"CHESTERTON, DROP THAT PEANUT!" Supergranny roared.

"SHACKLEFORD, SPIT OUT THAT MEATBALL!" she barked.

Talk about a shocked robot.

Talk about a surprised Old English sheepdog.

Talk about going from Life of the Party to Totally Embarrassed.

Chesterton dumped the peanut from his sensor, turned off his lights and beeper, and pretended he was invisible.

Shackleford spit out a revolting half-eaten meatball and stuck her head under a high-backed chair. She thinks we can't see her with her head under a chair.

"Sadie, honey, I can explain," Victoria's rich, rolling voice emerged from the thicket of mystery writers around Chesterton.

"Chesterton and Shackleford are so adorable," she said.

"And they were having SUCH fun," said the bearded mystery writer holding Chesterton.

"And we hated eating in front of them," said the meatball-throwing mystery writer.

"And we thought a few nibbles wouldn't hurt," said the flowered-dress-with-huge-hat mystery writer.

"And everyone's been SO ANXIOUS to meet you," said Victoria, pulling Supergranny further into the room.

Supergranny decided to be gracious about it. She smiled.

Fifty mystery writers thawed a little.

She laughed.

Fifty mystery writers smiled and went back to waving their toothpicks in the air.

"I know you folks didn't realize they're on strict gumdrop-and-dog-food diets for their health," she said. "Of course, THEY KNEW," she added, glaring at the bingers, who still pretended to be invisible.

That broke the ice and Victoria began introducing all the mystery writers to Supergranny, who kept telling them she'd enjoyed their books and was SO GLAD to meet them in person, while they kept telling her they were DELIGHTED to meet her after all they'd heard about her cases.

"Actually, I'm so relieved to see you're all safe that I really don't care WHAT those stinkers ate," Supergranny whispered to Victoria at the first lull.

"We found the rodent who has been threatening you, but we lost him and were so worried he'd come after you all and — wait a minute. Where's Olivia?"

"Oh, she's here somewhere," Victoria said. "See, there's her walking stick leaning against the table."

"Thank heaven," Supergranny said. "We think he's desperate and —"

"At least she was here a minute ago," Victoria broke in.

Supergranny frowned.

"OLIVIA!" Victoria called, looking around the room.

"OLIVIA!" Angela, Vannie and I called, threading through knots of mystery writers.

"OLIVIA!" Victoria called, looking under the table just in case.

"She's gone," Victoria said slowly. "But where?"

"I don't know," Supergranny said grimly. "But I'm afraid I know why."

# 12

"We have to move fast," Supergranny said. "I suspect Lionel has lured Olivia away, and the sooner we find them, the better.

"Shackleford and Chesterton, *front and center*," she yelled. "We need all hands, paws and grippers."

Shackleford and Chesterton snapped out of their invisible act and lined up in front of Supergranny faster than you can say "Cling, cling." They weren't about to dawdle, considering her mood.

"Here are your jobs," Supergranny said. "Pay strict attention. I can only go through this once.

"Angela — brief Victoria. Bring her up to date on the case. About Barklett. The Billy Goat. Chasing Lionel. The works. And do it fast — try a Three-in-One."

I was glad I didn't draw that job. Who could describe this case in only three sentences? In one minute? On the other hand, Angela once did a Three-in-One on Europe's Thirty Years' War[1], so I guess anything is possible.

---

1.  *Supergranny 3: The Ghost of Heidelberg Castle,* Page 14.

"Vannie," Supergranny went on, "take Shackleford and check out the women's rest room. Maybe we'll luck out and find Olivia there."

"Chesterton, round up the mystery writers and get them to the table. I need to question them about Olivia.

"Joshua, go downstairs and ask Fred if he saw Olivia leave."

Everybody scattered, and I dashed downstairs to find Fred.

Polly's was even more packed than before.

The aisles were clogged with people coming and going and hailing waiters and talking with friends. Worse, it seemed like about 48,000 waiters were racing around, all dressed in tuxedos like Fred's.

I finally gave up the search and went up front to the reservation desk to wait, figuring sooner or later he had to come back. I hoped.

It made me nervous just standing around with Olivia missing, but I figured it was smarter than wandering around Polly's all night, playing "Which Waiter is Fred?"

It worked. Two minutes later, here he came sailing toward the reservation desk, beckoning to the Party of Five behind me.

I dived between him and the Party of Five and asked whether he'd seen Olivia.

The good news was that he knew her because she always came to the Mayhem Mystery Club Meeting with Victoria.

The bad news was that she'd left.

"She left before you came in with Ms. Oglepop," Fred said, waving the Party of Five to follow him to a table.

"Just after the phone call,' he said over his shoulder.

"Wait a minute! What phone call?" I asked, chasing him and getting all tangled up in the Party of Five.

Fred stopped suddenly and our Party of Six crashed into him.

He seemed annoyed.

"Ms. Charmain received a call shortly before you arrived," he said in an extremely formal, headwaitery tone. "I transferred it upstairs to the Mayhem Mystery clubroom. A short while later, she left. Alone.

"Now, if you'll excuse me. I have ninety-two people waiting for dinner."

    *         *         *         *

Upstairs, things were a mess.

Fifty mystery writers, including Victoria, were seated at the long table. As soon as they'd finished voting on new members, Supergranny had told them about Olivia's disappearance.

The idea was, maybe one of them had overheard her say where she was going.

It looked like a rotten idea, because they'd gone so bonkers about having a *real* mystery to work on that their imaginations had swamped their brains.

True, they *wanted* to help.

"The window," Dangle-Earrings said. "Out the window by the snack table and along the ledge to the fire escape."

"Olivia went *out the window*?" Supergranny asked, as Victoria screamed and ran to the window to look out.

"Supergranny," I said, pulling her sleeve.

"No, NO!" Dangle-Earrings cut in. "I meant she *could* have gone out the window. Like Cleopatra Copyrot in my last book. When *she* was trapped above a restaurant she — "

"Thank you very much," Supergranny cut her off. "But

did anyone actually *see Olivia leave?*"

"Switched clothes with the waiter and slipped out through the restaurant," said the bearded peanut-popping writer. "Meanwhile, the waiter, disguised as one of us, is sitting right here at the table."

Everybody looked at everybody else. Nobody spotted a waiter disguised as a mystery writer.

"Supergranny — " I said, pulling her sleeve again.

She ignored me.

"You saw Olivia leave *disguised as a waiter?*"

"Nothing's impossible," the beard answered. "I used it in 'Nightmare Fast Forward'." A deposed Yugoslavian prince was stuck in — "

"Thank you very much," Supergranny cut him off. "But let's stick to facts. Did anyone actually SEE Olivia leave?"

"FRED DID!" I shouted. "OLIVIA GOT A PHONE CALL," I plowed on. Now that I had the floor, I was determined to keep it. "FRED TRANSFERRED THE CALL UP HERE, THEN OLIVIA LEFT THROUGH POLLY'S FRONT DOOR JUST BEFORE WE CAME IN."

Everyone stared at me.

"THAT'S ALL!" I shouted.

"Oh, yes, now I remember," said Flowered Dress and Huge Hat. "I remember Olivia taking a call by the snack table while everybody was playing with Shackleford and Chesterton."

"Did she do or say anything before she left?" Supergranny asked.

"No," Flowered Dress and Huge Hat answered slowly. "I saw her bring her walking stick back to her place at the table. But I didn't see her leave. I went back to watching Shackleford chase meatballs. I thought Olivia was watching,

74

too."

"Instead — " Supergranny began.

" — she left," Angela completed her sentence.

"But Olivia ALWAYS takes her walking stick when she goes out," Victoria said. "It's part of her image. And handy when the pavement's slick. And for hailing cabs. And warding off muggers."

"So why did she leave it?" Vannie asked.

"Why walk all the way from the snack table to put it beside her place?" Angela asked.

"It's as if she were trying to tell us something," I said.

"As if she were leaving us a message," Vannie added.

"CLING, CLING!" Chesterton went at the word "message." He raced to the walking stick, all blinkers flashing.

"Message! Of course!" Supergranny said, grabbing the walking stick. "Olivia left us a message." She unscrewed the gold Wrigley Building and shook the ebony walking stick.

A Polly's Supper Club napkin fell out, with scribbling on it.

We all crowded around Supergranny, and I got a glimpse of the scribbling before my view was blocked by a wall of backs and elbows.

It was an address . . . 5327 Wackley.

# 13

"But Wackley is *our* street . . . " Victoria said slowly. "That address is *next door.*"

"On the left?" Angela asked excitedly. "When you're facing your building, is it on the left?"

Victoria nodded.

"That's where somebody watched us through the curtains!" Angela exclaimed.

"Right," Vannie said. "When we were on the steps finishing the Famous Four Black Female Writers quiz."

Vaguely, I remembered, we'd thought a neighbor was watching because we were too noisy. But all along, maybe he was spying on Victoria's house and *us!* And last night, when our cab got to the Charmains'. Someone was watching then, too!

"And I saw Lionel on the sidewalk as our cab pulled away to the zoo," Angela added.

"Who lives in that building?" Supergranny asked.

"It has three apartments," Victoria said. "A young couple lives upstairs, and a playwright lives in the basement. I don't

76

know who lives on the main floor. Somebody new moved in a month ago."

A chill swept the room. It was creepy to think of sicko Lionel right next door to the Charmains'. Spying on them. Following their friends. Creepy. Disgusting. Dangerous.

The phone rang. It was for Victoria.

"If it's Lionel, play dumb," Supergranny hissed. "Don't let him know *we* know his address."

It was Lionel, all right.

We could barely hear his scratchy voice as we crowded around Victoria. Olivia's voice, however, came over loud and clear. From somewhere in the background she was yelling, "I'M ALL RIGHT, VICTORIA! I'M ALL *RIGHT!*"

Victoria grabbed a Polly's Supper Club napkin and motioned frantically for a pen. Forty-nine mystery writers tried to hand her one. She grabbed a felt-tip and jotted notes on the napkin.

Finally she stopped writing. "Don't hang up," she said quickly. "Let me talk to Olivia! Don't hang — "

She slammed down the receiver. "The vile little rat hung up. These are his instructions," she said, handing the napkin to Supergranny. "He says follow them to the letter . . . for Olivia's sake."

Supergranny adjusted her bifocals and read aloud:

1. Don't call police.

2. Go home. Find paper in front hall. Sign it.

3. Take signed paper and all copies of *Artist's Revenge* to Wrigley baseball field, Addison Street, Gate D. Alone. At Midnight. Tonight.

4. Put *Artist's Revenge* and the signed paper in the planter just to the left of the gate.

"You're the boss, Sadie," Victoria said when she'd finished. "How do we spring my sister? And stop this vicious little vermin?"

Supergranny glanced at her watch.

"With teamwork," she said. "OK, everybody, back to the table. We need everyone's help. Are you all with us?"

Fifty mystery writers, Angela, Vannie and I nodded. Shackleford barked. Chesterton beeped.

"Good," Supergranny said with a grin. "What a team! Now, here's the plan . . . "

\*        \*        \*        \*

After a quick run-through of the plan, Supergranny moved on to casting.

"First, we need someone to play me," she said.

Three seventyish female mystery writers stepped forward.

Woman One had a gray bun on top of her head just like Supergranny's.

"Perfect hair," Supergranny said.

"Except that she's six-foot-one, and you're five-foot-five," Victoria said. "That wouldn't fool Lionel in thick fog."

Supergranny moved on to Woman Two.

"Right height. Right weight. Right walk," Supergranny said. "In the right clothes, we could pass for twins."

"Except that she's Japanese and you're not," Victoria said drily. "And her hair is black."

Supergranny moved on to our last chance: Woman Three.

"Gray hair. Right size. Right walk. Perfect," Supergranny said.

The woman smiled and we all thought the part was cast until Shackleford walked past and she sneezed. And sneezed again. And sneezed and sneezed and sneezed and sneezed.

"Sorry," she gasped. "My allergies. Allergic to dogs, you know. *AhhhhhhhhhCHHHHHOOOO!*"

"Drat," Supergranny said.

"*AhhhhhhhhCHHHHHOOOO!*" the woman sneezed.

Casting was *not* going well.

Then Woman One saved the show. She whispered something into Supergranny's ear.

"By all means, take my bifocals," Supergranny said. "And here, take my shoes," she added, pulling off her Stars-and-Stripes tennis shoes. And my yellow apron," she added, pulling off her apron with the big "SG" on the front.

Woman One grabbed everything and pulled Woman Two toward the rest room, while Supergranny fished her spare bifocals out of her purse.

In five minutes they were back.

Woman Two was wearing Supergranny's bifocals and Stars-and-Stripes tennis shoes with Supergranny's yellow apron over her dress. She was also wearing Woman One's hair. That's right. Her gray bun. Her hair.

Woman One was wearing a scarf around her head. "I'd flip my wig to save Olivia," she said with a grin. "And I did."

Her Supergranny-style hair was a wig!

And now that Woman Two had IT along with Supergranny's bifocals and other stuff — presto! — a Supergranny double!

Never mind that Woman Two was Japanese and Supergranny was English-Scottish-German-French-Welsh-Indian-Irish. With the same bifocals, clothes and hair, they could pass for twins. From a distance. If you squinted.

Next, they had to cast me.

The youngest male mystery writer got the part. Luckily, he was short. Not as short as I am, but short. "And I did

79

a lot of acting in college," he said. "They taught me to do short."

The other parts that called for pizza deliverers and smoochers were filled quickly. A few people dashed home for trench coats, rain hats and boots for Supergranny and me, an ax and other props we needed.

In thirty minutes we were ready.

Supergranny stood at the purple door with the schedule:

9:45 p.m., Wrigley Field Squad — Thirty mystery writers dressed as themselves gathered at the door. Every five minutes Supergranny dispatched another group of three or four of them to catch the El or a cab to Wrigley Field.

Their job: Lurk in the shadows and protect Victoria.

10:30 p.m., Charmain House Guards — Twenty mystery writers posing as pizza deliverers, messengers, and passers-by lined up. Every five minutes Supergranny sent a group of four to Wackley.

Their job: Infiltrate the Charmains' block. Get into Lionel's building if possible.

11 p.m. — Victoria left for home with Supergranny, Angela, Vannie, Shackleford, Chesterton and me. I watched from the window as they climbed into a cab in front of Polly's. Of course, it wasn't really me down there. Mystery writers were posing as Supergranny and me. I just hoped it fooled Lionel.

11:10 p.m. — The Mayhem Mystery Club's secret dining room is deserted except for Supergranny and me. We put on our borrowed boots, turned up our borrowed trench-coat collars and pulled the brims of our borrowed rain hats down over one eye, taking a minute to admire ourselves in the mirror.

Then we flipped off the lights and quickly walked down the stairs, across Polly's and out into the rainy night.

# 14

We let our cab go a block from the Charmains' and lurked in a shadowy corner with a view of the Charmains' and Lionel's buildings.

The street was quiet.

Misty air draped the streetlights with slivers of rainbows. Traffic murmured on Lake Shore Drive, a couple of blocks away.

Supergranny lit a match.

I blew it out.

She lit another match.

I blew it out.

Inside the Charmains', Shackleford barked three times, stopped, then barked three more times, signalling that they saw the match and knew we were outside. Passers-by and Lionel would think it was just common, ordinary dog-barking. We hoped.

A pizza delivery car screeched to a stop in front of Lionel's. The bearded, peanut-plunking writer hopped out, carrying a pizza. He played the part perfectly because he had delivered pizza to pay the rent until his mystery became a bestseller.

He rang the bell, then disappeared into Lionel's building. He would pretend to deliver a pizza to the young couple upstairs, then hide in the hall until time to spring Olivia.

A couple sat down on the steps two doors from Lionel's and pretended to kiss. It was the dangle-earringed writer and her mystery-writer ex-husband. They were supposed to drag out the kissing until time to spring Olivia.

A mystery writer disguised as a man walking his Doberman strolled down the sidewalk and turned the corner into the alley to hide.

Three figures appeared on the Charmains' roof. They were mystery writers Victoria had led through the back door and up to the roof. Stealthily they crossed to Lionel's roof to wait.

The Charmains' door opened.

A shaft of light cut down the steps to the stoop.

Victoria, carrying a briefcase, stepped outside. She turned and waved to Angela, Vannie, Shackleford, Chesterton, Pseudogranny and phony me.

They waved back, making as much hullabaloo as possible to convince Lionel they were staying home while Victoria went to Wrigley Field alone.

He'd made a big point of that: She had to go alone. The door closed.

Victoria took a deep breath and started down the steps.

A cab pulled up in front of her. The driver was a mystery writer who looked just like a real cab driver because he drove a cab to make ends meet until his mystery hit prime-time TV.

So far, everything was going right. Victoria was there.

The cab was there. We were there. The writers were there.

Then things went wrong.

Victoria didn't get into the cab. She walked right past as though she didn't see it.

"Victoria!" Supergranny whispered to herself. "Get in the darned cab!"

Victoria was already to the corner.

The mystery-writing cab driver didn't know what to do. He started to follow her, then must have figured that would tip Lionel off that he wasn't acting like a normal cab. He screeched to a halt. Someone pulled the curtain back from Lionel's window. Someone was watching.

"Agghhh," Supergranny said under her breath. "The cab's going to wreck the whole rescue."

The cab-driving mystery writer was having the come-aparts.

He didn't know WHAT to do. He started after Victoria again, then screeched to a halt, leaving tire marks on the pavement while Supergranny pounded her forehead with her fist and groaned.

Flowered Dress and Huge Hat saved the show, slipping out of the shadows where she'd been hiding until "Spring Olivia" time.

"SO sorry to keep you waiting," she called gaily, pretending to be a neighbor who'd called the cab herself. "TO O'HARE AIRPORT," she shouted. "HURRY!"

The cab took off. Lionel's curtain dropped back into place.

"Whew!" Supergranny sighed. "That was close. I just hope Lionel didn't recognize her as one of our mystery writers. But why didn't Victoria take the cab as planned? I *hate* it when people don't stick to the plan!"

"But, Supergranny," I said, "maybe it's not her fault. Maybe Lionel has changed his instructions."

"Could be," she answered. "We'll just have to do the best we can. After her!"

We darted through the shadows after Victoria, who was already a block away.

*          *          *          *

She was headed for the El.

"Lionel *must* have called her with new instructions," Supergranny whispered. "He must have told her to take the El. Watch your rear. He may be following."

I looked over my shoulder in the murky darkness. If the turkey was back there, *I* couldn't see him.

At last Victoria got to the El platform and stopped. We walked right past her and leaned against a post a few feet away.

She glanced our way and lifted an eyebrow in a silent "hello.".

Supergranny lifted an eyebrow, then looked away.

I lifted an eyebrow. At least, I *tried* to lift an eyebrow. I *can* lift just one eyebrow, but it's the right one, which was under my hat brim. The left one is harder because they both lift, but since nobody could see the right one under the brim anyway, what difference did it make?

Never mind. Forget the eyebrows. The El thundered in.

Victoria hopped onto a brightly lit empty car, and we took the car behind her, still scanning the platform for Lionel.

Our car was empty, except for a woman wearing a light green uniform, a Cubs windbreaker and leather tennis shoes with the laces untied. She stared ahead blankly, looking very, very tired.

Just before the El pulled out, five more people rushed across the platform and clambered into the car behind us.

Was one of them Lionel?

"Check them out; I'll keep my eyes on Victoria," Supergranny whispered. *"Casually!"*

Casually, I turned to peer at the car behind us. I didn't think one of them was Lionel, but it was hard to tell because the walls of the car blocked part of the view and two of the people were standing in the way. In fact, they were walking this way. In fact, they were crossing into our car.

A foot-high sign said, "DO NOT STAND BETWEEN CARS AT ANY TIME" in English and Spanish, but they'd taken their Stupid Pills that morning and on they came.

They slid open the door of the car behind us and balanced on the hitch to slide open our car door. The noise of the train spilled into our car, then cut off as the door banged shut behind them.

"It's not Lionel," I whispered to Supergranny, who was still scoping out Victoria's safety. "Just a couple of muggers."

Actually, that was unfair. How did I know they were muggers?

Just because they had spiked orange hair . . .

Just because they had sickly pale skin like people on strict diets of barbecued potato chips . . .

Just because they sneered . . .

And swaggered . . .

And shouted . . .

And swore . . .

That didn't *guarantee* they were muggers.

For all I knew, they were undercover cops or Lionel's legmen or dedicated young actors on their way to a Punk

Party. Or some of our mystery writers carrying their disguises too far.

Whoever they were, they swaggered and swayed their way to the front of our car and into Victoria's. Supergranny and I braced ourselves to move if they bothered Victoria, but they swaggered on past and swayed through the sliding door.

With that mini-crisis past, I stood up to get a better bead on the others in the car behind us. I swayed in the aisle, pretending to read a "Phone for Your Personal Horoscope" ad and had a clear view of the three people in the other car — two women in long, black gowns and a bent, old man. If one of them was Lionel, he had a great disguise.

"Joshua," Supergranny whispered. I looked around. Victoria scratched her head, her index finger pointing toward the exit.

"This is our stop," Supergranny said, jumping up. If Lionel was watching, our getting up first made it less obvious that Victoria had bodyguards.

We stepped onto the platform as Victoria did and crossed in front of her, still pretending to be strangers, of course.

The two women in long dresses and the bent, old man got off. The tired woman got off. Everybody but the orange-haired muggers got off. It was as if we were all heading to the same party.

It was ten minutes to midnight.

The El clattered away. The only sound was our footsteps crossing the platform to the stairs.

# 15

"I don't like it," Supergranny whispered, as we led the pack down the stairs. "We're a stop short of Wrigley Field, which puts us blocks from our Wrigley Field Squad," (She meant the mystery writers hiding at Wrigley Field's Addison Street Gate D.)

"And if all these people are working for Lionel, the odds aren't so good," she added. "I wish we had Shackleford, at least."

So did I, so did I.

The four El passengers — the tired woman in the green uniform, the two women wearing long, black gowns and the bent, elderly man — were right on our heels.

Victoria was falling behind.

"Speed up. Try to shake them," Supergranny whispered.

We sped up. They sped up. They stayed right on our heels.

Victoria was now a half-block behind.

"Slow down. Maybe they'll pass us," Supergranny hissed.

We slowed down. They slowed down.

Victoria had stopped beside a trash can.

We stopped, turned around and stared at Victoria. The four El passengers stopped and stared at us.

Victoria was rummaging through the trash can! She pulled out something and looked at it.

Then she turned around and ran back up the stairs to the El.

Now what?

If we ran after her, we'd tip off Lionel, wherever he was, that Victoria was *not* alone. Not to mention what message it would broadcast to the four people on our heels if they turned out to be Lionel's henchmen.

On the other hand, how could we just let Victoria dash off to meet a crazy revenge-mongering artist? Alone? At midnight?

"Oh my, we've goofed," Supergranny said loudly. "We got off at the wrong stop. We're going to have to go back to the El."

"Excuse me," she said, pushing between the two women in the long, black gowns and walking briskly after Victoria.

That sounded too lame to fool anybody, but since I couldn't think of any way out myself, I was in no spot to criticize.

"Excuse me," I said, following her. My heart pounded as I pushed between the tired woman and the bent, old man.

Were they Lionel's goons? Would they come after us?

They came after us. Fast.

Supergranny and I broke into a run.

They broke into a run, fast as greyhounds around a track. Never have I seen two women in long gowns run so fast. Or a tired woman. Or a bent, old man.

Supergranny and I sprinted up the El steps. They sprinted after us.

Victoria stood in the shadows on the platform as another El rocketed toward us and screeched to a stop. As the doors opened, she moved forward.

A man stepped out of the first car and walked quickly toward Victoria. Without breaking stride he grabbed the briefcase from her and moved toward the still-open door of the next car.

"It's Lionel. He's getting back on the El," Supergranny yelled. "After him."

She brushed past Victoria and took a flying leap at Lionel. She grabbed him around the knees, and they both crashed to the platform, inches from the train. I threw myself on the briefcase, trying to wrench it from his hand.

His elbow jabbed into my stomach, knocking the wind out of me, just as Victoria and the four people behind us piled on.

"Got him!" yelled the women in the long gowns.

"Got him!" yelled the not-so-tired woman in the green uniform and the unbent, old man.

"Got it!" yelled Victoria, snatching the briefcase.

I rolled off Lionel.

Supergranny had him pinned. The other four held his hands and feet. They weren't working for Lionel! They were on our side!

Victoria stood up and raised her briefcase with her *Artist's Revenge* manuscript above her head like a trophy.

"Sadie and Joshua, may I introduce the four newest

members of the Mayhem Mystery Club. They weren't at the meeting tonight, but after I got a call from Lionel at home changing plans, I sent them an SOS. And here they are!

"And you, sir, I presume, are that vile little vermin, Lionel!"

He scowled as we pulled him to his feet and struggled as we took the El to the next stop and marched through the deserted streets.

Supergranny and Victoria led. Next came the women in the long gowns on either side of Lionel, each holding him by an arm. The unbent old man, the untired woman in the green uniform and I brought up the rear.

We crossed a narrow street and suddenly, fat, round, beautiful Wrigley Stadium loomed in the darkness.

On we marched, crossing the empty sidewalk straight to the planter beside Addison Street Gate D.

Supergranny pulled out her whistle and blasted an "all clear."

Suddenly, throngs of mystery writers surrounded us. And the midnight air at Wrigley Field rang with their cheers.

\*  \*  \*  \*

We had Lionel.

"Operation Guard Victoria" was a success.

But what about "Operation Spring Olivia?"

We had to get back to Charmains' house to find out.

A white limousine, owned by a mystery writer who'd had a string of bestsellers, slid to a stop beside us.

We climbed into the limo, with the women in the long gowns still clutching Lionel. Supergranny, Victoria and the unbent, old man rode backwards facing them, and the untired woman in the green uniform and I sat up front with the driver.

The other mystery writers scattered to their cars, pizza vans, pickups and bicycles, to line up behind us.

"Olivia had better be safe at home," Victoria said to Lionel as we pulled away from the curb. "She'd better be all right."

Lionel just stared at his knees.

# 16

I asked Angela to write up "Operation Spring Olivia" since she was there and I wasn't. Her first report was 137 pages, so I asked her to boil it down.

Here it is:

## OPERATION SPRING OLIVIA
### By Angela G. Poindexter

Victoria, Pseudogranny, Phony Joshua, Vannie, Shackleford, Chesterton and I took a cab from Polly's Supper Club in Chicago's Loop at approximately 10:58 p.m., arriving at Charmains' at 11:17.

Our assignment:

1. Make sure Lionel saw us going into Charmains'.
2. Make sure he saw Victoria leaving to meet him alone.
3. Rescue Olivia after Lionel left.

The night was wet and gloomy, and most of us were feeling pretty gloomy ourselves. Victoria was worried sick about Olivia. All Victoria really wanted to do was break down Lionel's door, but that was just too risky for Olivia's sake. We had to get rid of Lionel first.

Shackleford and Chesterton were also feeling down, because of all those hors d'oeuvres they'd eaten. Vannie and I were a little down ourselves, mostly because of Olivia, but partly because we were worried Shackleford might throw up in the cab.

Fortunately, Pseudogranny and Phony Joshua were feeling talkative and time passed fast in the cab.

Pseudogranny, as you know, is Japanese. Actually, she's American, but she was born in Japan, married an American soldier in 1950 and became an American citizen in 1955. She'd just visited Japan and had fascinating stories to tell about meeting great nieces and nephews who were the age *she* was before World War II.

Unfortunately, there isn't time to go into that here, so I'll save it for the "Japan's Teenagers — Then and Now" in-depth report I'm doing for school next fall. I like to interview real people for my reports whenever possible.

Unfortunately, there's also not time to tell you about Phony Joshua, who had just graduated from Loyola University in Chicago with a degree in theater. It's a pity because some of you might be interested in studying theater at Loyola yourself in a few years and might like to hear of it.

HOWEVER, I'm supposed to STICK TO THE POINT, so suffice it to say when we arrived at the Charmains', Shackleford had managed *not* to throw up in the cab and had pulled herself together enough to bark as planned when we got out. The idea was to create a commotion so Lionel could see we were all back at the Charmains' as he'd directed. (Of course, *we weren't* all back because Supergranny and Joshua would be coming later to hide at the corner, but you know that already.)

The first thing we saw when we piled into the Charmains' hall was an envelope that had been slipped under the door.

You'll remember one of Lionel's directions had been: "Go Home. Find paper in front hall. Sign it."

Victoria tore open the envelope. It was a contract:

To Whom It May Concern:

I, Victoria Charmain, relinquish all rights to the enclosed manuscript, *Artist's Revenge.* I will not seek to publish the attached material nor refer to it in conversation, press interviews, memoirs or any other way whatsoever.

Furthermore, I admit that *Artist's Revenge* was never my creation, but material I plagiarized from another unnamed source.

Signed _____
                         Victoria Charmain

Date _____

It was a lie, of course. Victoria hadn't stolen the story from anybody, which is what "plagiarized" meant. But to Lionel's twisted little mind, it might stop her from coming after him later.

Victoria was so worried about Olivia that she just sighed, signed, and stalked upstairs for her manuscript.

The rest of us went to work.

I went into the kitchen to boil Minute Rice for Shackleford. Boiled rice helps settle her stomach after a binge.

Vannie hooked Chesterton up to a battery charger in the living room to recharge his circuits, which were going goofy from the peanuts. (So far, only his lights were dim and his beeper weak, but prevention is the best cure.)

Pseudogranny and Shackleford took their posts by the bay window, waiting for a signal from Real Supergranny and Joshua. Poor old Shackleford was doing her best, even though she *was* sick as a dog.

Meanwhile, Phony Joshua opened the back door for the mystery writers assigned to "Spring Olivia."

Five minutes later Victoria marched back into the kitchen and dumped three copies of *Artist's Revenge* on the butcher's block counter. "Here they are," she said with a scowl. "The only known copies in captivity."

Then she called the young couple and playwright who lived in Lionel's building. "I don't have time to explain," she told them, "but can you do me one favor?"

They agreed.

By now mystery writers were slipping in the back door and crawling through the windows. While Victoria took some of them to the roof, Vannie and I stuffed the three copies of *Artist's Revenge* into Victoria's briefcase.

First was an old, yellowed, typewritten copy of the original story written some thirty years before. Second were the computer disks of the rewrite she'd been working on the past few months. Third was the only printout she'd done from the disks.

The phone rang.

Vannie answered it and raced upstairs for Victoria, while I dumped the rice into a pie plate for Shackleford.

Lionel was on the line and was changing everything.

Instead of Victoria taking a cab, she had to take the El.

Instead of going to Wrigley Field, she had to get off at the stop before it, turn right, and keep walking until she saw a trash can with a red paintbrush sketched on it. She was supposed to search through the trash can for new instructions. Yuck.

"Terrific, wonderful, just delightful," she said sarcastically. "Sadie's out there ready to follow me in a cab, half the Mayhem Mystery Club is waiting to protect me at Wrigley Field, and I'm going to be on the El by myself *blocks* away.

Phony Joshua saved us.

"THE NEW MEMBERS!" he shouted.

We all stared at him.

"THE NEW MEMBERS! I'VE GOT THEIR NUMBERS RIGHT HERE!" He pulled a folded paper from his wallet. As membership chairman, he had to call them about being accepted into the club.

Victoria looked at the list. "They haven't been to any meetings yet, because they were just OFFICIALLY accepted tonight," she said slowly.

"So Lionel won't recognize them if he *does* see them," I added.

"And four of them live just a few blocks away!" Phony Joshua yelled, already punching numbers on the phone, while Victoria shoved an El map under his nose.

Mercifully, two mystery-writing sisters who played violas in the Chicago Symphony Orchestra had just walked in from a concert. They said they'd be on the next El, no questions asked, and defend Victoria if necessary. "By the way," they added, "we're honored to be accepted into the Mayhem Mystery Club."

Next, Phony Joshua reached a mystery-writing waitress

who'd just gotten off work. She was as agreeable as the viola players. It didn't faze her a bit when Phony Joshua warned her of danger. "Anything for a fellow mystery writer," she said.

Last, he got a mystery-writing retiree out of bed. "Anything to help Victoria Charmain," he said. "She's my idol. I'm out the door."

Phony Joshua slammed down the receiver and grinned.

Shackleford barked in the living room. It was the signal: Real Supergranny and Joshua were at their posts.

The next act was about to begin.

Victoria picked up the briefcase, and we all walked to the front door. Victoria hugged Vannie and me and signaled "thumbs up" to Pseudogranny, Phony Joshua, Shackleford, and Chesterton, who was still plugged into the battery charger.

She squared her shoulders, stepped outside, and you know the rest of *that* story.

Meanwhile, "Spring Olivia" moved into high gear.

*       *       *       *

We stood behind the shutters and watched.

First, we watched the stuff you already know about: Cab-driving mystery writer pulls up. Victoria ignores him. Cab driver confused. Flowered-Dress mystery writer jumps into cab. Cab takes off. Victoria walks to El.

And then, the street was still.

This was it. Match point. Crucial test.

Was Lionel watching our little drama from his window, never suspecting Olivia had tipped us off where he lived?

Would he fall for our ruse?

We had our doubts.

"Maybe they're not even there," Vannie whispered.

"Maybe he took Olivia to some warehouse or something."

"Maybe he's got a whole gang guarding Olivia," Phony Joshua whispered.

"Maybe they're armed to the teeth," Pseudogranny added.

"Naaah," I whispered, trying to rev up the troops. "He's always been a loner, so he's probably acting alone now. Besides, *we* have our own gang." I thought of the mystery writers on the roof. The pizza-delivering mystery writer hiding in Lionel's building. The Doberman-walking mystery writer in the alley.

Suddenly, a shaft of light spilled down the steps of Lionel's building and was gone.

A dark figure in a gray raincoat moved stealthily down the steps and melted into the shadows after Victoria.

It was Lionel!

"Hooray!" Vannie whispered. "All *right*! Hooray!"

We waited five minutes. He didn't come back, and nobody else left. Shackleford finished her rice, Vannie uplugged Chesterton, and Phony Joshua picked up his ax.

"Now!" I whispered.

Shackleford gave three sharp barks, the signal for OPERATION SPRING OLIVIA — *ATTACK!*

We streamed out the front door and up the steps to Lionel's building.

I pressed the bell for the young couple's apartment upstairs.

Nothing happened.

Vannie pressed the bell for the playwright's basement apartment.

Nothing happened. Had they gone to sleep and forgotten the favor they'd promised Victoria?

Phony Joshua raised the ax to batter down the door.

Just in time, the upstairs people buzzed to release the lock. Pseudogranny turned the knob, and we slipped into the dark hallway as the playwright, a little slower on the draw, buzzed to let us in, too.

All clear, so far.

The hallway to Lionel's apartment was deserted. We tiptoed to his door. All was quiet on the other side. Not a rustle. Not a murmur. Not a peep.

Maybe Lionel *had* taken Olivia somewhere else. Or maybe there *was* a gang on the other side of the door lying in wait. Maybe they *were* armed to the teeth.

Now was the time to find out. Phony Joshua raised the ax.

I tugged Shackleford's leash. She gave one sharp bark. It was the signal. SPRING OLIVIA — *ATTACK TWO!*

The ax tore into the door, and we pushed inside. Dozens of mystery writers and a Doberman crashed through the windows. They spread through the apartment checking closets, the bathroom, and under the bed for Lionel gang members.

But there weren't any gang members — just Olivia, tied and gagged, but otherwise good as new.

"My stars, you nearly gave me a coronary," she gasped as I pulled the gag from her mouth. "I'd dozed off. Is Victoria all right? Where is she? Did you catch Lionel? I'd advise you to keep Shackleford away from that Doberman.

"And thanks! Nice rescue. A bit noisy, but nice."

We left six mystery writers and the Doberman on guard in case Lionel returned. The rest of us took Olivia home.

That concludes my portion of the report. AGP

# 17

It's me, again, Joshua, back in the limo with Lionel staring at his knees as we drive through the night, trailed by a convoy of mystery writers. He'd clammed up and refused to say squat about Olivia, which made us all nervous and gave Victoria the major fidgets.

Finally we got to the Charmains'.

Victoria was out of the cab and up the stairs before you could say *"Artist's Revenge."*

And Olivia flung open the door.

Never have I seen two sisters so happy to see each other. They laughed and hugged and danced and sang, while 53 mystery writers crowded around, laughing, hugging, dancing, singing and congratulating each other on cracking a real crime at last.

It was a great celebration, but it was too soon.

Too soon, because it created mass confusion just as we were pulling Lionel up the steps.

We didn't need mass confusion at that point. In fact, we probably didn't need fifty-three mystery writers at that

100

point. Ten would have been plenty. Even five.

The worm saw his chance and went for it.

Faster than you could say "Mayhem Mystery" he wrenched free and darted into the swarm of mystery writers, pushing and shoving until he got a mystery-writer avalanche tumbling down the steps. I glimpsed him springing over the banister as I fell.

"GRAB HIM!" Supergranny yelled, sliding toward the sidewalk in a tangle of mystery writers.

I tried but I was on the bottom. Luckily, there were just a few steps, and nobody landed very hard, but in the dark it was very confusing.

"Thrrrrummmp, thrrrruummmp," something fat and hairy bounded over my head. "Clingclingclingclingcling," something cool and sharp zipped over the pile of mystery writers.

We *finally* finished falling down the steps and set about pulling each other up and checking each other out and saying things like, "Are you all right?" "I'm fine, are you all right?" "Where is the scuzzball?" and "Did he get away?"

It was like a knot trying to untie itself and I was sure Lionel would be halfway to Rockford before we were vertical.

But he wasn't.

And once again, cheering and laughter filled the night.

For there was ol' Lionel backed against a light pole not twenty feet away.

Chesterton had him by one pant leg and Shackleford had him by the other, jerking her head from side to side and growling as though she regularly ate crooks and spit them out for breakfast, which of course was a lie.

Sitting in front of them was a Doberman watching the

show with his head cocked as though he wondered, "What's going on? You guys need any help?"

And, meanwhile, the crowning touch . . . a Chicago police car skidded around the corner, cut its siren, and stopped.

"All right, all right, ALL RIGHT!" Lionel screamed. "You got me! I surrender! OKAY???"

*     *     *     *

After the police hauled Lionel away we all gathered in the gallery to review the case.

"Angela, how about a Three-in-One," Supergranny asked.

"You mean describe this *whole case* in only three sentences? In one minute?" Angela asked.

"Sure. Just the high points," Supergranny answered.

"You did it for The Thirty Years' War," Vannie said.

"But THIS is complicated," I quipped.

Everybody laughed.

"OK — I accept the challenge," Angela said. She took a deep breath, and was off:

"Lionel was jealous of Barklett, much like Roderick was jealous of Alphonso; so when Lionel, who worked part-time for a publisher, read Victoria/alias Penelope Pickwith's *Artist's Revenge,* he stole its ideas to ruin Barklett's career.

"Many years passed; then eight months ago, he read in "People Magazine" that the former "Penelope Pickwith" was now the famous Victoria Charmain, and he worried that *Artist's Revenge* might be published after all, connecting him with Barklett's disaster; so Lionel moved here, managed to meet Olivia and when he found out that Victoria WAS publishing the old story, tried to scare her off

102

by pretending the book's Alphonso had come to life, even slipping a message into the walking stick while visiting Olivia, and when Supergranny, a well-known detective, showed up he tailed us and knew the jig was up when he saw us with Barklett at the Billy Goat, so he panicked and lured Olivia away, hoping to get Victoria's only three copies of the manuscript.

"He probably thought she'd be too scared to rewrite it or tell the police because of the paper she'd signed saying she'd 'plagiarized,' not to mention that Lionel was on the loose and might return to terrorize them at any time . . . BUT we all worked together, and squashed his scummy scam!"

Everybody laughed.

"But I still don't understand how Lionel wound up next door," Pseudogranny said.

"That was my fault," Olivia answered. "After Lionel did my portrait six months ago, he started dropping in for coffee."

"Always when *I* wasn't home," Victoria pointed out.

"Right, but I didn't think about that at the time," Olivia went on. "Anyway, I happened to mention the apartment vacancy over coffee."

She shivered. "I never dreamed he'd use it to spy on us and shake down Victoria. I didn't start to get wise until last night, when the kids suggested someone might have used the book's ideas to destroy a rival."

"I thought you were going to tell us something then, but you didn't," I said.

"You told Lionel instead, didn't you, Olivia?" Supergranny asked quietly.

"I did ask him about it," Olivia answered slowly. "I

103

left an urgent message on his answering machine. When he finally called me back at the Mystery Club meeting, he said he didn't understand what I was talking about. But he insisted we meet immediately to clear up any misunderstanding.

"He sounded so innocent . . . I felt so ashamed of suspecting such a prominent artist that I almost didn't leave the message for you in the walking stick . . ."

We all shivered, except the Doberman-walking mystery writer, who snickered instead, then threw back his head and laughed.

"I'm sorry," he gasped, brushing tears from his eyes. "I just remembered how funny my Doberman looked going up that ladder."

Lionel's windows were six feet off the ground, and some of the writers and the Doberman had climbed ladders to crash through the windows.

That got the others arguing about the case's funniest parts.

"My Doberman was DEFINITELY the funniest part," the Doberman-walking mystery writer insisted.

"No, no, the funniest part was when I slid down a rope from the roof to crash through the window and slid too far," a roof-brigade mystery writer insisted.

"I slid all the way to the ground, landed in the geraniums, and had to climb up a ladder to the window." She doubled over with laughter. "After all that time waiting on the roof, ziiiip, right past the window into the geraniums."

The mystery writers partied on, but Shackleford and Chesterton, who'd had a very rough day, crawled under the rubber plant in the bay window and went to sleep. The Doberman, who turned out to be a very gentlemanly dog, joined them.

Vannie, Angela and I tried to pry Supergranny away to go back to our suite at the Barclay, but no luck. She was in heaven rehashing the finer points of the case with fifty-four mystery writers, counting Victoria and the four new members.

So, we wrapped up in quilts, grabbed throw pillows and settled down with Shackleford, Chesterton and the Doberman.

We needed all the rest we could get.

It would be daylight in four hours, and Supergranny would be raring to get on with her beloved Chicago Hit List.

After all, we'd been here two days, and we hadn't even been to the aquarium, the Sears Tower or a Cubs game — not to mention a show at the Schubert.

We *knew* what was coming tomorrow. Except for cheeseburgers at the Billy Goat, we hadn't even *started* the major optionals.

# ABOUT THE AUTHOR

Beverly Van Hook grew up in Huntington, West Virginia, graduated from Ohio University, Athens, and now lives in Rock Island, Illinois. A journalist who wrote for national magazines before turning to fiction, she has received numerous writing awards, including the Cornelia Meigs Award for Children's Literature and the Isabel Bloom Award for the Arts. She is married to an advertising executive and has three children and an Old English sheepdog exactly like Shackleford.

# ABOUT THE ARTIST

Catherine Wayson grew up in Iowa and now lives in Huntsville, Alabama, where she is a full-time professional illustrator and free-lance artist and photographer. Her paintings and photographs have appeared in juried shows nationally and throughout the Midwest.